Dear Reader,

This book is labeled "A Classic Novel of Love" because it is indeed "a classic," originally published in
1983, and a "novel of love," shorter and narrower in
scope than my more recent novels.

It was originally written under the Billie Douglass
pseudonym. Since readers now know my real name,
I am using that on this reissue. The only other
change you will find is the cover design. The title is
the original one, as is the story within.

I hope you enjoy reading AN IRRESISTIBLE
IMPULSE both as much as I enjoyed writing it, and as
much as I enjoy rereading it today.

Barbara Delinsky

Recent Titles by Barbara Delinsky from Severn House

AN IRRESISTIBLE IMPULSE

Barbara Delinsky

severn
House

This title first published in Great Britain 2001 by
SEVERN HOUSE PUBLISHERS LTD of
9–15 High Street, Sutton, Surrey SM1 1DF.
This first hardcover edition published in the USA 2001 by
SEVERN HOUSE PUBLISHERS INC., of
595 Madison Avenue, New York, NY 10022,
by arrangement with HarperCollins*Publishers*, Inc.
Originally published in paperback format only 1983 in the
U.S.A. by Silhouette Books, under the pseudonym *Billie Douglass*.

British Library Cataloguing in Publication Data

Delinsky, Barbara, 1945-
  A time to love
  1. Love stories
  I. Title
  813.5'4 [F]

  ISBN 0-7278-5673-1

20045378

MORAY COUNCIL
LIBRARIES &
INFORMATION SERVICES
F

All situations in this publication are fictitious and
any resemblance to living persons is purely coincidental.

Printed and bound in Great Britain by
MPG Books Ltd, Bodmin, Cornwall.

one

SHORTLY AFTER NOON ON A BRIGHT FALL Wednesday, Abigail Barnes was taken into custody. She was escorted down the center aisle of the crowded courtroom by a somber-faced sheriff's guard. Whether it was apprehension or excitement that threatened her steadiness she wasn't sure. But she was oddly grateful for the firmness of the hand at her elbow, guiding her through the large black leather-sheathed doors to the stairway that wound to the ground floor of the Windsor County Courthouse.

"The van is waiting out front," the burly guard clipped as they started down the creaking steps.

Abby simply nodded, too concerned with matching his pace on the narrow stairs to say a word. Reaching the door, she was whisked through, then momentarily exposed to the noontime sun as the guard hurried her down the short granite path before inserting her into the dark blue van standing at the curb. She was barely seated when the door slid shut with a jarring bang. Her gaze flew questioningly to the uniformed driver as the guard returned to the courthouse.

"Where . . . ?" she began, looking wide-eyed and helpless enough to evoke sympathy.

"He's gone to get the others. Then we'll be on our way."

"The others?" she asked softly. "So there *were* others?" It had been impossible to tell the fate of those taken from the holding room before she herself had been called.

"Two others," the guard informed her smugly. "We're getting there." Satisfied, he turned his attention to the gaggle of curious bystanders scattered on the lawn, the sidewalk, the street. Following his gaze, Abby seemed to notice the crowd for the first time.

"What *are* they staring at?" she whispered self-consciously, the question simply an expression of dismay to which she didn't expect an answer. She received one nonetheless.

"You." The guard tossed the single word back over his shoulder, then said no more.

Abby shivered in anticipation of what was to come. Lowering her head and settling more deeply into her seat in a futile effort to escape the eyes beyond, she yielded to amazement as she reviewed the events of the morning.

It had seemed that she'd been sitting for hours when in fact it had only been ninety minutes. Closing the medical journal in her lap, she shifted on the splint-back chair in an effort to get comfortable, then raised her eyes to study quietly her companions in the small jury room.

Propped straight in identically unyielding chairs, these men and women represented a cross section of the Vermont she'd come to know well.

No one could deny the subtle tension in the air. Each person in the room had heard the judge at the

2

start of the morning's session and knew that, should he be chosen as a juror for this trial, his freedom would be sharply curtailed for the next three weeks. Three weeks. To Abby, the thought was not as odious as it might have been a year earlier. Then there had been no Sean Hennessy in her life, pressuring her for a commitment she simply couldn't make. The chase hadn't even begun then. Now it tired her. Three weeks of captivity might offer an odd but welcome freedom.

Her lips toyed with a mischievous smile as she took a breath and sat back. She recalled the moment earlier that morning when the judge had addressed the gathered group, explaining the mechanics of a locked-up jury, asking to see those who, for one reason or another, couldn't possibly serve. A good half of those present had stepped forward, each taking a private turn before the judge, offering his best excuse and a plea for sympathy. In the majority of cases it was forthcoming. Judge Theodore Hammond knew the importance of weighing civic responsibility against emotional hardship. His jurors would have to be in top shape to absorb the barrage of testimony presented to them. The Bradley case promised to be a headliner. It wasn't every day that the grown son of one of the state's most prominent citizens stood trial on a charge of kidnapping.

The soft hum of conversation brought Abby's attention back to her fellows, several of whom carried on discussions among themselves. Others had buried themselves in books or magazines. Still others stared distractedly out the windows at the sparkling fall morning, much as she might have been tempted to do had her attention not been caught by a pair of warm gray eyes.

Slowly, she turned her head toward her viewer. He was every bit the man with a rakishly rich head of tawny brown hair, a face full of character, and a build that spoke of virility combined with grace. Abby was intrigued by the contrast he presented to the average man in the room. He was younger, probably not yet in his forties, charmingly casual in tan corduroy slacks and a matching blazer patched at the elbows, and he wore a certain air of worldliness she found captivating.

As he lounged against the sill of one of the four ceiling-to-hip windows, he seemed much more relaxed than the others. She wondered whether he too might have a secret reason for appreciating a three-week hiatus from routine. But she averted her eyes, feeling strangely shy when the stranger's brow furrowed in puzzlement. Perhaps he too wondered . . .

Abby's gaze was one of many that shot toward the door as it opened to allow for the court officer's appearance.

"James Szar-Szarcylla . . . ?" He read from his list, faltering slightly, relieved when a middle-aged man in a worn brown suit recognized the pronunciation and rose to be led upstairs to the courtroom.

The tremor of a collective sigh whispered its relief through those remaining. Venturing another glance at the man by the window, Abby was pleased to find that he too had detected the murmur and found similar amusement in it.

For it was an odd waiting game they played. This was the third full day of jury selection. Of fourteen jurors needed—the usual twelve plus two alternates—nine had already been chosen. And there was no way of knowing how many had been added to the roster from those interviewed this morning. It wasn't unrealistic to assume that at any time now the judge would declare a successful impanelment of the jury and announce the prompt dismissal of those not chosen to serve. *That* was the obvious prayer of most in the room.

Not so Abby. Granted, the thought of being sealed off from the world for a period of three weeks had disadvantages for her, too. There were numerous commitments, both professional and personal, that she'd very much miss. Yet she somehow felt it to be a worthwhile trade.

With a sigh, she drew back the soft cuff of her blouse to reveal the oval face of her slim gold watch. Eleven-thirty. A busy time at the office. Janet would be covering for her. But then would come lunch and the good Dr. Hennessy wouldn't settle for Janet. He'd be after Abby. Always after Abby. If only she returned his love . . . but she didn't. And, nuisance that he was notwithstanding, she simply couldn't tell him to buzz off. For one thing, he was her boss. For another, she was too kind a soul to hurt him. After all, they'd been dating for months, and she did care for him deeply. There had to be another solution.

"Abigail Barnes . . . ?"

Her head shot up as her name echoed loudly from the door. Returning from distraction with a startled blink, she realized that this one moment of truth, at least, was at hand. Composing herself, she tucked the journal into her bag, rose from the chair, and walked forward. She was aware of every eye in the room following her, but hesitated before the court officer only long enough to spare a sidelong glance at the man by the window. Answering his wink for good luck with a shy smile of her own, she crossed the threshold and followed her leader toward the stairs.

It was the last smile to cross her lips for a while. One simply didn't smile while seated on the witness stand facing three sober judges, opposing teams of

stern-faced lawyers, a packed gathering of spectators and media representatives, and an intent-eyed
defendant. One simply filled in one's name, address,
and occupation when asked to, elaborated wherever
it was requested, and answered as honestly as possible any other questions posed.

At only one point had Abby been concerned that
her forthrightness might remove her from consider-
ation. It had been when the judge had rocked back in
his oversized chair and narrowed his gaze on her.

"Now, Miss Barnes, we come to the sticky matter
of pretrial publicity. As you know, the purpose of a
sequestered jury is to protect the jurors from any
force that might possibly influence them during the
course of the trial. We have no control, however,
over what you may have picked up in newspapers or
on television during the past weeks and months.
Please answer me as honestly as you can." He had
levered himself forward then, stressing the gravity
of his plea. "Have you either heard or read anything
about this trial prior to your coming here today?"

Frowning, Abby had wondered how any thinking
person in the state could have arrived here in total
ignorance. The very fact that there had been a
change of venue from the northern county where
the crime was purported to have taken place was evidence of the wealth of publicity that had surrounded the case. The press had been concerned
with little else for days.

"Yes," she admitted with soft trepidation. "I've
followed the story." She held her breath, waiting,
but he seemed neither surprised nor discouraged.

"Could you tell me what you remember hearing
or reading?"

Feeling awkward for the first time, all too aware of
the defendant sitting not five yards away, she kept
her eyes on the judge. "I've read that Derek Bradley,

the defendant, was arrested and charged with the kidnapping of his former lover, who claims that he took her to an isolated cabin and kept her there for several weeks. Actually, most of what I've read has dealt with the publicity that will surround the trial once it begins."

The judge nodded. "I understand. Now I want you to consider whether you feel you've formed an *opinion* based on what you've read. In other words, do you already have an assumption as to the guilt or innocence of the defendant?"

Lowering her head, Abby had pondered the question. Then she looked back at the judge. "No, I don't believe so. It's the role of the court, not the media, to determine the guilt or innocence of a person."

"Then you feel you'd be able to hear the evidence with an open mind?"

"Yes," she responded with a confidence she felt.

Still sober, the judge looked toward the lawyers. "The court finds this juror indifferent. Mr. Weitz?"

Indifferent, it appeared, was a good thing to be if one wanted to serve on a jury. Within minutes, she had been duly sworn in and committed to the state for the next few weeks of her life.

The van door slid open abruptly, jolting Abby back to the present. Two people climbed in, the guard shut the door firmly behind them and took his place riding shotgun up front, and the engine came to life. Inching its way along a narrow path between parallel lines of parked cars, the van gained speed only when it rounded the town green and found clear space to proceed westward.

Taking a deep breath, Abby looked hesitantly at her fellow passengers, a man and a woman, both seeming as stunned as she.

"Jurors?" she ventured softly, her eyes wide with caution.

It was the woman, middle-aged and innocuous, who spoke first. "Afraid so. You too?"

"Uh-huh. I'm Abby Barnes."

The older woman nodded her head. "Louise Campbell."

Abby smiled in acknowledgment of the introduction, then turned toward the man, who was slightly older than Louise and that much more grim. "Hi," she said, tipping her head sideways.

The man hesitated before somehow managing a perfunctory smile for her benefit. His voice was as solemn and nearly as begrudging as the dark cast of his eyes. "It's Tom Herrick. Nice to meet you. I guess. Wish it were under other circumstances."

Abby's smile was more genuine this time. "It's a shock to the system, isn't it?" she asked rhetorically. Then, reluctant to push her luck, she quietly redirected herself to Louise. "What will you be missing?"

For a woman who had given her name so laconically, Louise Campbell was surprisingly fast to fill Abby in on what was obviously a gnawing issue. "I'll be missing my job—I'm a dietician for the Springfield public schools. Mostly though I'll be missing my husband. Honestly, I could brain that man." Her frustration came through loud and clear. "*I* might have easily been excused for reasons of his health. He has high blood pressure and numerous other little ailments, and he's on a very restricted diet." She scowled and adopted a faintly mocking tone. "But he gave me a lecture last night about my responsibility to this state. He all but forbid me to use him as an excuse. I think *he* wants a vacation."

Abby would have chuckled had she not seen the keen worry on the woman's face. "I'm sure he'll be fine." She tried to offer comfort, a token thing since she knew neither this woman nor her husband. "Is there anyone else at home with him?"

"No. He's alone. And he'll probably put on three pounds a week eating everything I've denied him for the past two years."

"Nah," Abby scoffed playfully, "maybe he'll surprise you and behave himself."

"Hmmmph . . ." was the woman's only response. And as quickly as the conversation had begun it ended.

Taking a deep breath, Abby looked from one shuttered face to the other, then turned her attention to the passing scenery. Lord only knew there would be time aplenty for conversation with these two during the next few weeks. And the others . . . who would *they* be? Would there be anyone with whom she'd *really* be able to talk?

Not, she mused, that she was dependent on friends for her own emotional stability. To the contrary. She saw herself as being abundantly self-sufficient, living alone and enjoying the solitude. Every major decision she'd made in her twenty-eight years had been truly hers. Yet, perhaps it was precisely this independent lifestyle that heightened her appreciation for the companionship of others. Warm companionship. Stimulating companionship. An intelligent mind off which she might bounce her thoughts. Interesting thoughts to bounce off her own mind.

Unbidden came the image of one tawny-haired man. What if *he* were chosen? It might be fun, she mused idly. And interesting. He obviously had a sense of humor. *That,* she sensed, was going to be a necessity in the days and weeks ahead.

The turn of the van from the main road onto a private one brought more immediate thoughts to mind.

She'd been familiar with the route they'd taken, had driven it many times herself—toward Killington to ski, toward Rutland to shop. Yet she'd never taken this side road. They hadn't been driving for more than five minutes. Logistically, it would be right.

To either side, towering stands of pine and hemlock crowded the shoulder of the road, leaning eagerly forward for a better view of the van and its passengers in much the same way the people in town had done. Abby chased a strange eeriness from her mind as she kept her eyes on the road ahead.

And she was rewarded. For around the next seemingly endless bend appeared first a garden house, then a garage, then an absolutely huge and beautiful home with the simple legend "The Inn" emblazoned on its lamppost.

"This must be it," came the resigned rumble from Tom.

"Not bad," Louise allowed reluctantly.

Abby, however, couldn't restrain her pleasure. "It's charming," she breathed. "Where did it ever come from? I've never *heard* of an inn being tucked away so successfully!"

The van had stopped and conversation would have done the same had not the officer who opened the door by Abby's side appreciated her enthusiasm. When he grinned, she knew she had an ally. "Nice, isn't it? And southern Vermont's best-kept secret to boot!"

Taking the hand he offered, Abby stepped from the van to admire better her surroundings. "Is it a *public* place? I mean, can *anyone* stay here?"

"Usually . . . yes," he answered, lending a hand to the older woman before turning toward the house. "Now . . . no." There was a certain finality to his tone, a chill reminder of their purpose. Anxious to hear whatever he might say, Abby kept pace with him on the broad flagstone path, her slim-heeled pumps tapping a rhythmic cadence, her full skirt swirling just below her knees. She was unaware that the driver of the van had unobtrusively taken up position behind Louise and Tom and now followed watchfully.

"One of the reasons this inn was chosen for you folks," the first officer went on, "is that it *is* secluded and unknown, so to speak. There'll be no other guests staying here for the duration of the trial." Pulling open the large screen door, he stood back. "Hope you're hungry. Sybil's a terrific cook."

At the moment Abby was indifferent to the enticement offered, for she was suddenly besieged by warring emotions. On the one hand she was thrilled to find herself in the gracious foyer of a sprawling mansion set on acres of land; on the other she felt no freer than a bird in a cage. One part of her felt pure delight at the thought of vacationing at this inn; the other was appalled at that delight, given the sobriety of the occasion. She felt excitement and trepidation, anticipation and apprehension. Hungry? . . . Not quite.

"Ah!" came a gentle male voice. "You're here!" Abby turned to meet her host, a man whose kind expression was in keeping with that voice. "I'm Nicholas Abbott. And welcome to The Inn."

Nicholas Abbott extended his hand to each of them in turn. His warmth helped dispel that chill she'd felt moments before. Dressed casually in slacks, an open-necked shirt, and a golfing sweater that buttoned from waist to hip, the innkeeper was as gracious as the setting he'd created. He spoke slowly, reassuringly, as if understanding the unsureness his guests had to be feeling.

"My wife, Sybil, and I hope to make your stay here

as comfortable as possible. We're really a self-contained entity. But if there's anything you need and can't find, please feel free to ask either of us ... or your trusty guards." He cast an eye toward a large room branching from the foyer. "Uh-oh. Looks like your trusty guards are hungry." The men in question stood looking longingly toward the end of the room that was beyond Abby's view. "Let's go have lunch," her host suggested gently. "The others have just begun. I'm sure they won't mind pausing for further introductions."

His words brought home the fact that, if this was the beginning for Abby, there were others for whom it was the third day of sequestration. Curious, she followed Nicholas Abbott toward the adjoining room.

The two court officers stood aside to let the small troop enter. Abby found herself in an enormous room, the front half of which was comfortably furnished in typically New England parlor style, the rear half of which was an elegant dining room dotted with casually set tables for four, at which were scattered nine other jurors and two additional court officers.

"Hear ye!" Nicholas made a lively gesture of clapping his hands for attention. It was far from needed. The newcomers had captured every eye in the room the instant they'd entered it. "We've got another three to add to the group." Speaking more softly, he extracted first names from Abby, Louise, and Tom, then went carefully around the room giving similar identifications to each guarded face.

Abby couldn't have remembered eleven names in one round if she'd tried. The most she could do was to note a fairly even sexual split and the predominance of jurors older than herself. Just one woman appeared to be close in age, perhaps even a year or two younger. This woman's name she made a point to catch. Patricia. Blond-haired and fair-skinned, Patricia returned both her interest and the half-smile Abby was able to offer before being ushered to a free table.

Moments later, she found herself seated with her fellow new arrivals and a court officer, a woman who had quietly shifted her place setting to their table from that at which she'd begun the meal.

"I'm Grace Walsh." She grinned knowingly. "...Just in case you didn't catch the name the first time around. I'll be here with you throughout the trial."

"You mean that they don't give *you* any time off either?" Tom grunted in a tone just short of sardonic.

Grace shrugged off the question with a dismissing wave. "Oh, I'll probably have a morning or afternoon off every now and then, but for the most part . . . you're stuck with me."

Smiling, Abby took a closer look at this person with whom she was "stuck." In her late forties, Grace Walsh made a very proper appearance, with her brown hair anchored in a staid bun, her face devoid of makeup, her blue uniform fitting her ample body with just a hint of room to spare. Yet there was no sign of the grim matron in this woman, no clue to suggest that she might next be walking a criminal to and from a prison wagon. Rather, she seemed eminently approachable . . . so much so that Abby yielded to her own clamoring curiosity.

"Tell me, Grace," she began, helplessness written across her features, "how is this all supposed to work? I mean, I know that we'll be cut off from the outside world. But exactly how far does it go? There are those little day-to-day things that people do—laundry, phone calls, reading. How much of that will be affected?"

The kindness with which Grace responded did little to blunt her words. "Everything, I'm afraid. You'll come into contact with no one but courtroom personnel, your fellow jurors, those of us who'll be staying with you, and the staff here at the inn." She shifted her gaze to the waitress who approached bearing a large tray. "This is Katherine Blayne, the Abbotts' oldest daughter. She lives with her own family back in town, but she's here helping out every day." Then she turned to Katherine. "The stew tastes great!"

The eldest Abbott daughter grinned. "There's plenty more whenever you're ready." Lowering her tray onto a nearby stand, she transferred a basket of bread, a central vegetable dish, and individual salads to the table before returning with a large serving bowl and dishing out hearty helpings of a steaming beef stew. "I hope this is okay for you folks. If any of you have any dietary restrictions, please let us know. We'll be glad to make substitutions." Katherine glanced quickly at the table to make sure she hadn't forgotten anything and then returned to the kitchen.

"Hmmmph!" Louise scoffed softly as she eyed the heaping plate before her. "And I was worried about my *husband* gaining weight . . ."

Grace turned to Louise and said cheerfully, "One of the beauties of this place is the opportunity for exercise. There's a pool out back, but now that the end of September's here it may be too cool to swim. If any of you run, though, Ray over there"—she quirked her head toward the guard who'd driven the van and now sat at the table she'd left earlier— "would be more than glad to take you. He's a pro. Enters marathons and all. And the paths around this estate are ideal for running."

The thought held major appeal for Abby. She'd

been running since she first moved north and discovered that the fresh air—warm in summer, crisp in spring and fall, downright frigid though invigorating in winter—did miracles for the cobwebs that formed periodically in the private corners of her mind.

"I might just take him up on that," she quipped. "I have this funny feeling that after sitting in the courthouse seven or eight hours a day I'm going to need *something.*"

Her reference to the trial seemed to sober them all. As Abby listened for it, conversation in the room was sparse. Rather, there were the sounds of eating—silver touching china, the clink of glassware as it moved from table to mouth and back, an occasional cough. Eyes down, she focused on her lunch, eating absently, trying to tell herself that a certain awkwardness was only natural. After all, the people in this room had been thrown together through circumstances quite beyond their control. Each had his own life, his own friends, his own loyalties . . . and there were still two more jurors to be added to the unlikely assortment.

"When do you think the trial will begin?" she broke the silence on impulse to home in on Grace.

The woman raised her eyes skyward. "With any luck we'll get our jury completed this afternoon. If so, opening statements should begin tomorrow morning."

Nodding, Abby returned to her meal. Tomorrow morning. At least she wouldn't be waiting around as some of these others had done. Two more jurors. Her thoughts took a frivolous turn as she wondered again whether that enticingly human male with his casual stance and his amused expression would be one of the two. A surreptitious glance toward the other tables convinced her that he'd be by far the most attractive of the group.

Then her eye met Patricia's, and the other gave a meaningfully exaggerated yawn. So the group was as fascinating as she'd feared? Ah, well, there was always Scrabble, or a good book, or if worst came to worst, she could spend her free time writing letters to Sean.

She hadn't realized she'd chuckled aloud until Louise called her on it. "You don't seem as bothered by the situation as we are. No husband at home? Kids? Job?"

"Oh, yes," she replied softly, "I certainly have a job. But you're right. I don't have a husband or children to worry about. It makes a difference."

Evidently her frank concession was enough to quell the older woman's curiosity. There were no more questions asked. Indeed, the meal progressed in silence through gingerbread à la mode and a welcome pot of herb tea. It was only when the foursome prepared to leave the table that Grace spoke up.

"There's one thing I'd like to ask you all now," she began. "The judge will elaborate on this tomorrow morning, but let me say quickly that you aren't to discuss this case with anyone. That means no talks with each other after court or at night. I know it might get pretty tense holding it all in, but that's the rule. We ask that you honor it."

She'd ended on such an urgent note that for the first time the three nodded in agreement. "Good. Now then," she resumed more buoyantly as they headed for the lobby, "you've each been assigned a room. That's another nice feature about The Inn—private rooms for all. I think I'll have Mr. Abbott show each to his own. Clean up if you want. Take a rest. Then," she paused to look around for her quarry, "if I can corral my colleagues we can get down to the business of taking you back to your homes to pick up your things."

It wasn't until mid-afternoon that Abby finally arrived at her house. She was accompanied by another female officer, Lorraine Baker, who'd come to her rescue after Grace had taken off with Louise. It was quite an experience, she was later to muse, to walk through one's own house with a stranger in constant tow. But it was in keeping with the rules of sequestration that had been outlined earlier. *Nothing* was to influence her now—not the morning's paper which lay neatly on the kitchen table, nor the daily mail, which the policewoman dutifully sorted and censored, nor the best-selling novel, newly bought and ripe for the packing, that told the story of a psychopathic rapist.

Lorraine was at her elbow examining everything. Most things—clothing, cosmetics, blow-dryer— were easily approved and promptly stowed in Abby's canvas traveler. Other things, to her dismay, were vetoed. A headphone cassette system to run with was out, as was a portable radio or any other device for providing a musical accompaniment to relaxation. As Lorraine explained, there couldn't be any risk of an outside message "infiltrating by electrical means."

The phone rang three times. Each time Lorraine deftly reached it before Abby. That, too, was an experience. For when the first caller was identified as her neighbor, Cindy, and Abby extended her hand for the receiver, she was as amazed as her friend to hear Lorraine politely explain that though Abbey couldn't talk, Lorraine would be glad to relay the conversation.

Yes, Abby *would* be serving on the Bradley jury. No, she wouldn't be home again until the trial was over. Yes, it would be a big help if Cindy could call the medical center and tell them the news. No, Abby couldn't have visitors. No, she didn't want to cancel the mail, but would Cindy be kind enough to pick it up for her and sort through it for anything critical? Yes, she had everything she needed, and anything else could be picked up later by one of the court officers. Oh, and could she call Celeste O'Brien and ask her to take over her natural childbirth classes for the next few Saturday mornings? And Sean . . . would she be a sweetheart and call him for her?

As it happened, the last was unnecessary. For the second call, coming while the receiver was still warm, was from none other than the doctor himself. Had she *just* gotten home from the courthouse? She *what?* Who was *this?* And why *couldn't* Abby come to the phone?

Abby's expression warmed in amusement as Lorraine related one after the other of the questions Sean fired. Taking her cue from Abby, she humored him gently. Sean, however, was barely appeased when he finally hung up moments later.

"That was not a happy man," was Lorraine's wry observation.

"No," Abby mused as she gathered together several professional journals, some notebooks, pens and pencils, and the leisure reading that had finally been deemed acceptable. "I didn't think he would be." She sighed. "At least he can't blame *me."*

As she'd anticipated that morning, Abby most definitely sensed relief at the prospect of several weeks away from Sean. She needed the break; things had grown claustrophobic.

The peal of the phone wrenched her from her thoughts, though only for a minute. For it was Sean again, with a second round of questions. How long would the trial be lasting? Couldn't he see her—

even for a chaperoned visit? How could she possibly
be chosen to serve on a jury? After all, she was a
nurse and as such was in great demand!

Once again Lorraine fielded the inquiry with prac-
ticed flair, relating Abby's responses in those few instances when they were offered. For the most part,
Abby stood back and let her guard take the flak. If
she was truly to be "protected" during this experience, she reasoned impishly, shouldn't such protec-
tion begin at home?

With Sean off the phone once more, though, there
was little else to be done. The thermostat was lowered, the lights turned off. After a final check of the
house, Abby lifted her bags and helped stow them in
the wagon Lorraine had driven.

As the car moved ahead and the house fell behind, she was filled with the same anticipatory excitement she'd felt that morning in the courthouse.
She'd had her wish; she'd been chosen. Now she was
looking forward to the experience.

Later, back at the inn, unpacked and washed up and
changed into a soft silk shirtwaist, Abby headed
downstairs toward the living room, where cocktails
were being served. Cocktails. Two drinks per night
by decree of the judge, she'd been told only half in
jest. Therapeutic . . . if purely optional.

Pausing on the threshold of the room, she eyed
the reserved gathering. The jurors. Her counter-
parts. Somehow she felt discouraged by her impression of them as a subdued, even stoical group. Not
that merriment was called for, given the purpose of
their presence, but a certain conviviality might help
pass the time. Perhaps a drink or two would do won-
ders at that. . . .

"Lively crew, isn't it?" came a voice of conspiracy
close by her ear. Its deep velvet sound quickly con-

jured the image of a most intriguing man. Though she'd never heard him speak, the tone that warmed her now held that same spirit she'd seen etched in his features that morning. There was lightness, and a sense of adventure, plus a certain ability to take it all in stride.

Catching her breath and closing her eyes, Abby dared to hope in that instant that she might be right. Then, tempering enthusiasm with caution, she slowly turned.

two

AT CLOSE RANGE, HE WAS MUCH TALLER THAN Abby would have imagined, but he looked every bit as exciting as he had that morning. And if she'd feared the loss of his humor with his selection as a juror, she was quickly heartened by the vibrant sparkle of his eyes.

"Hi," she offered more breathlessly than she'd intended. "I wasn't sure you'd made it."

"Nor I you," he countered in quiet confidence. "Believe me, it's a relief." He cast a glance past her shoulder into the room. "I'm not sure about these others. . . ."

Abby's gaze joined his, her voice as low. "I know. Not too encouraging, is it?"

"To say the least. It's obvious they'd rather be anywhere but here."

"Not you?" she asked, turning to look pertly up at him.

His grin bore a hint of that air of conspiracy she'd heard in his voice moments earlier. "No more so than you."

His cocked brow seemed to invite her elaboration, but she wasn't quite ready to accept the invitation. Rather, she looked back toward the group, which stood in awkward clusters around the room. "It's a hardship for many of them, I guess."

"Not enough to be excused . . ."

"No, but still, in *their* minds, it may be an ordeal."

"Not in yours?" he reversed the questioning. She had no choice but to follow suit.

"No more so than in yours." She grinned, feeling suddenly and surprisingly happy. "I'm Abby Barnes."

A large hand was extended her way. "Ben Wyeth here. It's my pleasure."

In fact, the pleasure was hers. For his hand was warm and encompassing, his fingers confident in their grasp. And his smile . . . his smile did something very delightful to her insides. She could only nod more shyly and wait until he released her and spoke again.

"You *don't* seem at all disturbed at the idea of being locked away for three weeks," he began directly. "Why not? And don't tell me it's your duty!"

Abby laughed knowingly. "You've heard that one today, too?"

"More than once," he drawled, then grew more serious, "but tell me your reasons."

Of the many she'd analyzed in the course of the day, she chose the least personal and shrugged at its simplicity. "It's . . . an exciting opportunity. Something new and different, not to mention important." She blushed. "But even that sounds pompous."

"Perhaps," Ben acknowledged, "but I agree with you. This case will be a controversial one. To serve on its jury *has* to be a challenge."

A sudden thought returned Abby's attention to those in the room. "Is it complete . . . the jury? I was number twelve."

"I'm thirteen. Bad omen?"

To the contrary, she mused, but gave a shrug of coy innocence. "Who knows . . . and number fourteen?"

Ben put his hands on her shoulders and turned her to the right. Then he leaned forward, his mouth close by her ear again. "There. The gentleman in the green jacket."

Her eye easily found its target. "Oh, dear, how *could* I have missed him? I've never seen a blazer quite that . . . shade before!" she reflected diplomatically.

"It's called wake-up green. Charming, isn't it?" he quipped.

"Absolutely." It had to be the loudest thing she'd ever laid eyes on.

Reading her mind, Ben straightened. "I think I could use a drink. Come on. Let's go in."

The hesitancy Abby had felt when she'd first arrived downstairs seemed to have vanished. Taking confidence from Ben, she let him guide her between watchful groups of twos, threes, and fours toward the bar at the far end of the room.

"Bourbon and water," she prompted the bartender. Ben ordered his straight, then turned to study the jurors silently. Abby studied him.

His profile had a chiseled quality about it, his features strong, not quite perfect. His hair had a natural wave, with lighter streaks woven through cocoa to hint where one day there might be gray to match his eyes. Tonight he wore tan slacks and a brown tweed blazer, with a crisp white shirt which played up the last of the summer's tan.

"Here you go, folks." The bartender handed them their drinks. Abby accepted hers gracefully before following Ben's direction to a nearby window seat.

"What do you do in real life?" he asked, safely installing her in a corner of the bay and sliding down within arm's reach.

" 'Real life?' " She chuckled. "I like that." Then she spoke more quietly. "I'm a nurse."

"A hospital-type nurse?"

"An office-type nurse. I work with a pediatric practice."

"Nurse practitioner?"

Her eyes brightened. "You've heard the term?"

It was Ben's turn to chuckle. "I have a close friend who's a pediatrician. He swears by his nurse practitioners, depends on them to handle the less serious problems while he tackles the major ones. He's the first to sing their praises."

"Thank heavens for that!" Abby exclaimed. "We need all the help we can get when it comes to our image."

"You mean *your* doctors don't appreciate you?"

Abby's cheeks flamed as a picture of Sean flashed through her mind. "Oh, they do! And our patients do, too. But other people . . . well . . . it seems that I'm constantly having to explain that my job is different from that of a bedpan lady." She thought back to the morning's explanation. "Come to think of it, the judge was more solicitous than most. After I described my responsibilities as falling midway between those of a traditional nurse and a doctor, he wanted to be sure I could be *spared.*"

"And you can?"

"I'm here, aren't I?" she rejoined with a smile, looking up to find herself drawn into his gaze. It seemed a fine place to be lost just then.

"I'll drink to that," he declared as though sensing her thoughts again.

Abby joined him, sipping her drink absently. "But what about you?" she asked at last. "What do you do for a living?"

"I teach."

Her eyes widened. "Do you really?"

"Uh-huh." His lips twitched just enough to suggest that there was more to the story. She bit readily.

"Children-type teach?" she asked, borrowing his style, imagining him propped on a desk before thirty seven-year-olds.

Despite the look of indulgence on his face, he crushed that image summarily. "Young adult-type teach."

"College level?"

"That's right. I'm on the faculty at . . ." Feigning caution, he lowered his voice. ". . . uh, at the college across the river."

Loving his theatrics, Abby beamed. "You teach at Dart—"

"Shhhhhhh. More than once I've been accused of treason." He glanced furtively at the others. "And I don't particularly care to alienate these good citizens so early on in our association."

Unconsciously, she'd lowered her voice to match his. "But it's an Ivy League school!" she argued. "They should be proud of your association with it, regardless of whether it's in New Hampshire or Vermont. And besides, it's less than thirty minutes away!"

"Make that fifteen from where I live. And you're right. It's a fine school. But still," he sighed, "it's not in Vermont. These people have a unique sense of loyalty."

She shot a glance toward the citizens in question. It seemed none had moved beyond a shuffle to the right or the left. Her voice remained low. "In this case, I'd say it was martyrdom. Why *do* they look so disgruntled?"

Ben, too, noted the predominance of sober faces.

A drink in hand had done nothing to relax them. "They're not used to change, I guess," he remarked thoughtfully. "You have to admit that living up here is much more placid than life in the big city. We've both been *there!*"

Puzzled, Abby frowned and looked slowly sideways. "How did you know?"

When he looked back at her, he seemed startled, as though unaware at first of the assumption he'd made. His own brow furrowed beneath its casual thatch of hair. "Bourbon and water, I guess. It came so naturally to you."

She nodded, smiling her guilt. "That'll do it every time. Not that I drink often, mind you, but a fellow I dated through college had this thing for bourbon. I guess I developed a taste for it out of necessity."

"How about the guy? Taste gone bad?"

"A lonnnnnng time ago," she drawled without regret, amazed at the extent of her own relaxation. Benjamin Wyeth was an easy person to open to. Benjamin Wyeth . . . saying his full name, albeit silently but for the first time, struck a familiar chord. She couldn't quite place it.

"Have you ever married?" he asked gently, momentarily diverting her attention.

"No. . . . How about you?"

For the first time, he seemed to withdraw into himself. His eyes darkened fleetingly, his brows drew together. His voice took on a distant quality when he spoke. "I was married once . . . a long time ago. . . . My wife died."

"I'm sorry, Ben." Reacting on instinct, Abby reached to put her hand on his arm. "It must have been very painful."

As quickly as he'd gone, he returned to her, his eyes softer now, searching. "It was. It still is sometimes. We were young and idealistic. She died in a

fluke accident. I suppose half the pain was disillusionment—you know"—he forced a grin—"the it-
can-happen-to-anyone-else-but-us type of thing."

"Like serving on a sequestered jury?" she asked
softly, intent only on making him forget the past.

He nodded and smiled more naturally. "Like serving on a sequestered jury." Then he tipped his head
to the side in pensive query. "Do you live alone?"
Startled by the shift, she simply nodded. "Do you
mind it?"

She gave herself a minute to gather her thoughts.
"No. I kind of like it. I've always had roommates for
one reason or another—until now. Even after three
years, it's still a novelty. Besides, there are friends
and neighbors to keep me from getting lonely." At
work there was Janet, and even Sean when he wasn't
harping on the state of his heart. In her South Woodstock neighborhood there were the Alexanders—
Cindy and Jay—who had opened their home, their
hearts, and their minds to her when she'd first
moved north from New York. Then there were people like Marta, whose hand-woven shawls had
become *the* thing with which to warm one's shoulders on a chilly Vermont night. And Ted, whose
knowledge of Bach ran a close second to his exper-
tise on the winter slopes. And Andre, in whose bookstore she'd spent many a Saturday afternoon and
whose literary recommendations had brought her
that many more Sunday afternoons of pleasure.

"You've never wanted to live with . . . a man?"

Momentarily taken aback by the more personal
turn of the conversation, Abby took time to find the
right words. There was nothing to be defensive
about; she knew her mind where the opposite sex
was concerned. "No," she said gently, "I've never
wanted to do that. And it hasn't been simply a matter of principle. I never found anyone I care to spend

twenty-four hours a day with." She hesitated for a second. "I suppose it would be nice . . . with the right man. . . ." Her lips thinned as she thought of Sean. What *was* wrong with their relationship? Why couldn't she get excited about him?

"Ah-ah. There *is* someone," Ben teased. "I can see it in your eyes."

As she shook her head, her hair waved darkly by her shoulders. "No, there's no one." It was, in a way, the truth.

Far from convinced, her companion shifted on the window seat to stare at her thoughtfully. "It's strange. . . ."

"What is?"

"Your reaction to being here." His gaze narrowed, and Abby felt suddenly self-conscious. The voice that went on was deep and intense, surprisingly so for a man she'd taken to be easygoing. "You're looking forward to this just as I am. I could tell that the minute I saw you this morning. In that sense, we're different from the others . . . you and I." He paused to study her closely. "You live alone, so it's not a roommate you're trying to escape. And you have a job, a good job that interests you. So it's not as if you're dying for a vacation. . . . Am I right so far?"

"Uh-huh," she replied, intrigued by the analytic nature of his mind. He seemed to be solving a riddle, and enjoying every clue.

"Now . . . this business about a man. You're attractive, intelligent, and single. And you have to have known that this wouldn't be a 'swinging' time. So I ask myself *why* a woman like you would welcome an experience like this."

"I've already given you a reason."

"One," he reminded her with a teasing smile. "But I have this nagging feeling that there's another. You get a certain look in your eye every so often. Is it relief? I'd almost suspect that these three weeks are a kind of reprieve for you." He paused. "Now you're blushing. Am I close?"

"It's the bourbon," she argued, trying to stifle a grin. "What did you say you taught?" It had to be psychology.

"It's not the bourbon," he went on, clearly enjoying the banter. "You've still got the better half of that drink in its glass. And I didn't *say* what I taught . . . but it's political science."

"No kidding! That's a great field. Any specialty?"

"You're trying to change the subject."

"I thought we were talking about each other."

"No, Abby. I was talking about you—"

"Uh, excuse me, Dr. Wyeth, Miss Barnes." Both heads flew up to find the bartender standing before them looking decidedly awkward. "If you'd like to bring your drinks into the other room, I believe Mrs. Abbott has dinner ready."

Ben was smoothly on his feet, his hand at Abby's elbow drawing her up. "Thank you. I'm afraid we were . . ." he cleared his throat conspicuously, then looked back at Abby, ". . . wrapped up in ourselves."

It was only when the bartender turned to walk away that Abby realized the room was quiet . . . and empty. "How embarrassing!" she whispered, blushing more furiously. "I hadn't even noticed they'd gone!"

"That's because they're such a captivating group," he quipped.

"I don't know," she mused. "Maybe we're not being fair. After all, this is only the first night. We haven't given them much of a chance."

They'd reached the lobby and crossed through. At the entrance to the dining room, Ben spoke more quietly. "Maybe you're right. Perhaps we ought to separate during dinner and concentrate on getting to know the others."

But Abby suddenly realized she'd been looking forward to having dinner with *him*. "On the other hand," she hedged, lowering her voice to a stage whisper as they neared the tables, "I don't see that there's any rush. There'll be plenty of time—"

The thought was suspended in favor of a sheepish grin when three faces turned to regard her questioningly. Ben had made up his mind, she mused, and *that,* evidently, was *that.* There was nothing for her to do but accept disappointment graciously.

"May I join you?" she asked softly, aware that her escort had already pulled out the only free chair for her. Three quiet nods met her inquiry. Dutifully, she sat down.

All things considered, it could have been worse. The food was superb, a sole almondine that Abby found to be as good as any served in the finest restaurants at which she'd eaten. Vegetables and bread were fresh, and the chocolate truffle cake for dessert was more than she'd bargained for. Her quip about "needing that exercise after all," though, went over like a lead balloon.

It wasn't that there was hostility, but rather a pervasive wariness that inhibited conversation as nothing else might have done. While the upcoming trial must have weighed heavily on every mind there, no one dared discuss it for fear of violating the directive given earlier.

Nor was there significant talk of a personal nature, much as Abby tried to initiate it. She would have been interested to learn more about these people, their homes, their jobs, their families. But with each question came a simple and usually deadended response, offered in a tone that discouraged further inquiry. Had Abby not known better, she would have sworn the three had agreed upon a code whereby each chose to suffer in private.

Acceptable topics of conversation, on the other hand, were the outlook for the winter's ski-touring season, the oppressive price of home heating oil, and the ever-changing status of the American League pennant race. It wasn't that Abby was bored; she could easily chat along with the rest on these subjects. But there was something deeper at stake here, and her mind began to wander.

What *would* happen as the trial progressed? If the jurors were uncomfortable with each other as a group, how would they cope with the pressure that was bound to mount? Hours of intense concentration, days of sitting in the same chair listening to point after point of evidence, hearing first one side and then the other, with innumerable objections, overruleds, and sustained scattered about—for the first time Abby felt truly apprehensive. It was one thing to view the proceedings as a unique experience, quite another to acknowledge that the experience was apt to be grueling. Three weeks of service was a very long time. Would *she* hold up through it all?

There was, of course, one bright light on the horizon. He sat two tables to the left and was flanked by the court officer named Ray, one other gentleman Abby hadn't yet met, and Patricia, lucky Patricia, who seemed positively taken with Ben, if her rapt expression was an accurate index of enthusiasm. As a matter of pride, Abby refused to look for Ben's reaction. It was enough that she envied Patricia the company.

Nonetheless, she couldn't help but feel let down when he disappeared shortly after coffee was served. To her surprise, it was Patricia who moved to join her for a second cup when the others excused themselves as well.

"I missed you this afternoon," the younger woman bubbled quickly as she put her coffee cup down and slid into the free chair next to Abby. "I was hoping to catch you at some point. It's Abby, isn't it?"

Abby smiled, petty jealousies quickly forgotten. After the hour she'd just been through, a breath of fresh air had just wafted into the room. "That's right. . . . Patricia?"

"Patsy," the other nodded. "Did they get you home for everything you need?"

"Oh, yes. Lorraine supervised it all. It was an odd experience."

"I know. But you're lucky. I was sworn in yesterday and the waiting's been awful. At least today brought you and Ben." Her eyes lit up. "He's something else! I saw you with him before dinner and didn't want to bother you. You both seemed totally occupied with each other. Say . . . you're not attached or anything, are you?"

"To Ben?" Abby protested, suddenly cautious. "I just met him today."

"No, I mean . . . otherwise. You're not married . . . ?" When Abby shook her head, Patsy raced on eagerly. "Grab him! He's gorgeous!"

"Patsy—"

"No, I'm serious! You make a great-looking couple."

"This is a *jury!*"

"He's brilliant," she went on as though Abby had never spoken. "Do you know that he's a college professor? He didn't say where, and I had to all but pry *that* much out of him, but you should have heard the discussion he had with Bernie about the caste sys-

tem in India. Does he ever have facts at his fingertips!"

Abby had no doubt about that. "It sounds like
your dinner was a little more interesting than mine.
Who's Bernie?"

Barely stopping for a breath, Patsy was fast prov-
ing herself to be the antithesis of the other jurors.
"Bernie is Bernie Langenbach. He was the first juror
sworn in. Poor guy's been here since the day before
yesterday! He owns a restaurant in White River Junc-
tion."

"How about you, Patsy? What do you do?"

For the first time, the blond-haired woman spoke
slowly, but it was only pride that weighted her
words. "I work for the Eastern Appalachian Company designing skiwear."

"You *design* it? That's fantastic!"

Patsy nodded. "I enjoy the work." Then she grew
more mischievous. "And it gives me an excuse to
stay near the slopes. . . ."

Something in her eyes told Abby that her interest
wasn't purely in schussing. "Okay," Abby grinned,
liking Patsy more by the minute, "Let's have it. Who
is he?"

Smiling gaily, Patsy leaned closer. "He's a ski bum
and he's the most wonderful guy in the world! I
mean, he's smart and funny, and is he ever a good-
looker!"

"But can he ski?" Abby asked, holding her expression sober only until her friend laughed aloud.

"Can he ski?" She rolled her eyes heavenward.
"When he comes down that mountain, it is something to behold," she breathed in near reverence.
Then, in the instant, she started up again. "Boy, was
he annoyed when he found out I couldn't talk with
him."

Now the story sounded familiar. "He doesn't like

talking through an interpreter?" Abby asked, tongue in cheek.

"Not . . . a . . . bit!" Patsy loudly sucked in her breath, then let it out with similar gusto. "And do I love that possessiveness!"

Abby dissolved into gentle laughter. "You're amazing, Patsy. A change from the very staid folks I ate with tonight."

Sitting back in her chair, Patsy grimaced. "You mean Dean didn't thrill you with his opinion of the economy?"

"Uh-oh. You've heard it too?" It was slightly conservative, at best.

"Twice now. And Richard—he usually picks up with his plug for tourism. You know—it's a good thing that the rich *are* getting richer so they can afford to ski in these mountains. I hope you didn't try to argue with him," she added her warning, but it came too late.

"As a matter of fact," Abby moaned, "I did suggest something about all those *other* people who might like to ski—"

"And he clammed up?"

"Not another word."

Patsy nodded. "That seems to be the pattern. It's as though they're frightened of discussion. Not your Ben, though."

"He's not *my* Ben, Patsy. For all I know he's got some little coed stowed in his cozy condominium." All he'd said was that he'd been married once; he'd never ruled out a current lover. "And besides, I've got my own hands full just now."

"You do?" Patsy gleamed. "Tell me about him."

But before Abby was able to say a word, Nicholas Abbott approached. "Abby? You've got a phone call. It's your fiancé."

"My fiancé?" Who else? "But I can't talk, can I?"

34

"Grace is just finishing up with another call. She said she'd be glad to help you out."

Not quite sure if she wanted to be helped out, particularly given her annoyance at Sean's audacity, she hesitated.

"He says it's important," Nicholas added apologetically.

Sighing, she nodded. There was always that chance that Sean *did* have a question relating to the work she'd be missing during the next few weeks. She'd hardly given a thought to that, what with the events of the day, and she felt suddenly guilty. "Thank you, Mr. Abbott. I'll be right there."

Nicholas Abbott was barely beyond earshot when Patsy whispered hoarsely, "Your *fiancé?* Are you really engaged?"

"Not on your life," Abby murmured, standing and squaring her shoulders. Then she took a deep breath. "And I intend to tell him as much right now," she began boldly, only to be interrupted by Patsy's droll reminder.

"You mean, you'll have *Grace* tell him as much?"

"Uh-oh . . . well, yes. I mean, he knows we're not engaged and he'll have to realize that declaring himself my fiancé won't get him through any more directly!"

Patsy rose to walk beside her. "Go get 'im, Abby," she drawled when they reached the lobby.

Abby frowned and mumbled a low, "And here I thought I'd be free of all this . . ." as she spotted Grace in the office behind the desk, replacing the receiver from a call just completed. Then, her anger momentarily suspended, she watched Ben Wyeth nod his thanks to the court officer and head her way.

His brow arched roguishly. *"Fiancé?"* he taunted her in that soft drawl of his, and she knew he was about to add another clue to the puzzle. But before she could correct the misconception, he had nodded in salute and passed her on his way to the front door. She watched him helplessly, not quite sure why she felt so bothered, finally blaming it all on Sean as she took her turn with Grace.

When she emerged, there was no sign of Ben either on the front porch, where she'd assumed he'd been headed, or in the living room, where a handful of the others were sitting. Somehow she couldn't face joining them. With a sigh of defeat, she retreated to her room.

An hour later she sat propped against the headboard of the king-size bed wondering what to do with herself. Had she been at home, she would have read or listened to music, perhaps reviewed some notes for the following day's work. Now her mind was on the following day, but its focus was a very different kind of work.

It was only natural to be apprehensive, she told herself. After all, everything was so new. And Sean hadn't helped things with his argumentativeness. Even Grace had begun to despair toward the end of the call, after she'd explained the rules to him several more times. It wasn't that he couldn't understand them, simply that he wouldn't accept them. But that was *his* problem, Abby mused, shifting her feet to the floor and standing.

She paced slowly to the window then turned, finally sinking back into the cushioned armchair nearby. From the minute she'd seen this room, she'd liked it. Tucked up on the third and highest floor of the house, it had the same charm as the rest of the inn, perhaps even more with its dormer windows and tiny alcoves. Even now, as her eye wandered from bed to wall to dresser and rug, she felt totally at home and comfortable.

How had the others fared, she wondered idly? Did they too have handcrafted quilts on their beds, regional artwork on their walls, fresh flowers in the vases on their small sitting tables? This room was a palette of lavender, blue, and white. Were the others the same?

Against her better judgment, her mind wandered to Ben. Where was he now? Had the rooms been assigned in order of arrival . . . in which case he might be next door? She listened for any sound that might come from either of the adjacent rooms. . . . Nothing. Perhaps her neighbors hadn't come up yet. More probably, she decided with a frown, they were in bed. What about *him . . . ?*

With a soft exclamation, she jumped up and crossed the room to the nightstand by the bed. Within seconds, she had the front desk on the phone. Yes, the jurors were to be woken at seven. Oh, she wanted to run earlier? No, that was no problem. Ray would be going out at six. Was that all right with her? Fine, then; she'd get her wake-up call at ten before the hour. Was there anything else she wanted? A warm drink? An extra blanket? No? Well . . . good night, then.

When, after an hour of dropping notes to her family to tell them of her whereabouts, Abby finally fell asleep, her mind was filled with a myriad of thought fragments, not the least disturbing of which were about one Benjamin Wyeth, the caste system in India, and a nagging sense of something she'd forgotten.

That was it . . . the "J." Benjamin *J.* Wyeth. Dredged from her memory bank, it came to her the instant she awoke to three short rings of her phone. Benjamin J. Wyeth. It had to have been over a year now since his book had come out. She recalled Andre mentioning it one Saturday as he'd placed copies of it on the shelf. She hadn't seen it again, but then she hadn't looked. What was it on . . . not India . . . China, perhaps?

The question helped to keep her awake as she threw on her running suit, laced up her sneakers, and headed downstairs, wool hat in hand. Halfway down the last flight, her foot wavered . . . then continued more slowly.

"Morning," she said softly, testing a smile. It was a poor facsimile of the one she might have produced had it been two hours later. Usually she ran alone, with no one to witness her slow awakening. It was small solace that the others seemed as groggy.

Ray nodded silently, as did the juror named Brian. It was the final member of the running team, though, on whom Abby's attention stuck.

"All set?" he asked, his hair boyishly mussed and more sandy-hued in the morning's pale light.

"All set," she breathed and fell into step with the men as they moved toward the door.

Ray, the court officer-cum-runner, seemed most concerned with the female he had on his hands. "You run often, Miss Barnes?"

"It's Abby . . . and yes. Every morning."

They were on the front steps and descending. "Good. Why don't you and Brian move on ahead. I'll take up the rear with Ben."

Given her choice, Abby might have arranged things differently. She certainly hadn't expected to find Ben running, though in hindsight she should have suspected as much. He was too broad in the shoulder and too narrow in the hip to lead an inactive life. And since he'd been the first thought in her mind when she'd awoken that morning, this unexpected rendezvous might have been a boon. But then, she reasoned by way of consolation, she wasn't much up for talking yet. The sun had barely edged over the horizon, and she still had her own waking up to do.

Tugging the wool cap in place to ward off the morning's nip, she indulged in her usual stretching exercises before straightening to find all three men watching her.

"Is . . . is something wrong?" she asked, suddenly self-conscious as she looked from one face to the other. But her look turned to one of challenge when she recognized the male appreciation in their regard. "Don't *you* all limber up?"

"Not quite . . . that . . . way," Ben dared to reply, his hands on his hips, his eyes twinkling.

Ray wasn't as bold. "Let's go," he mumbled, waving Brian off.

Abby continued to stare at Ben for a final moment's censure before turning and starting out. "You know the way?" she asked Brian, who nodded curtly.

"Did it yesterday," was all he said. His eyes were on the path ahead, his concentration fully on his running.

Following his lead, Abby immersed herself in her own thoughts as she ran, much as she did every other morning. She found her pace and kept it, breathing evenly, pleased to find that with her lighter weight and more petite frame she kept stride with Brian easily. If these three thought they'd leave her behind, she reflected in amusement, they'd be in for a surprise. That very element of pride gave added bounce to her step.

The inn fell from sight as they wound through the trees on a path that seemed tailor-made for their purpose. Abby quickly saw the truth to Grace's claim that the jury's accommodations were ideal for recreation. Here there was no fear of contamination

Barbara Delinsky

from the public. Not once did she catch sight or sound of civilization. There was only the rhythmic slap of running shoe against pavement, the occasional sound of breathing, and, most delightfully, the morning sounds of the woodlands on either side.

Confident of her ability to run a six-minute mile, Abby used her watch as a measure of distance. Brian kept several paces ahead, seeming to know just which way to take at a crossroads, leading them in a general figure-eight pattern that was nearly the mile itself.

The sky grew lighter with the birth of the day just as Abby grew increasingly awake and aware of what that day would bring. One part of her would have been very happy to burrow in a mossy nook in the forest and then rejoin the runners at the same point tomorrow. But that was the coward speaking, she chided, knowing that her better part was filled with a subtle excitement.

And then, of course, there was the knowledge of Benjamin Wyeth pacing himself a distance behind. As the mile count rose from three to four, then to five, she grew increasingly distracted by that thought. Pride kept her from looking back; indeed, from the competitive angle, she was pleased to stay ahead. If only he weren't looking at *her* all the time.

As though summoned by her thoughts, Ben moved forward. "Not bad . . . for a girl," he quipped, falling into stride beside her.

Abby caught her breath and looked sharply up, prepared for battle. But his smile was so sincere that her flare of indignation fizzled. Contriving a frown, she simply shook her head in exasperation. If the truth were known, her usual limit was the rapidly approaching six-mile point. It occurred to her that she might soon *be* out of her league. Best she should concentrate on holding her pace steady.

40

But Ben's concentration was more inclusive. "Does your fiancé ever run with you?" he asked with nonchalance.

So much for steadiness, she mused as her pulse raced faster. Had that been on *his* mind all night . . . or was it an innocent question? A quick glance at his expression failed to enlighten her.

"Nope."

They ran a little further.

"You told me there was no one."

She waited until they'd crested a small rise. "There isn't."

Had she looked at him then, she might have seen him nod at the logic of it all. She had to wait somewhat longer for his verbal response.

"What's a fiancé?"

With a will to revenge the disquieting fact that he'd had free scrutiny of her for the past forty minutes, Abby ran on some before answering.

"In this case," she spoke between breaths, "it's a man who insists on making a pest of himself."

"Ahhhhhh . . ." He saw the light.

Simultaneously, the inn loomed ahead. The runners slowed gradually before reaching the front steps, each seeking his own walkaround, letting his legs readjust to a more natural pace. Coming to a full stop at last, Abby grasped the sturdy wood railing and stood for a minute to catch her breath. Then she pulled the wool cap from her head, thrust both hands through her damp hair to comb it back over her shoulders, and sat down to cool off before going inside.

Ben promptly slid down against the opposite railing and watched as first Brian then Ray excused themselves and disappeared. Then he straightened one leg, bent the other at the knee and leaned back.

"You're *not* engaged," he stated, looking at her askance.

"Nope." Angling forward at the waist, she grasped her calves and carefully flexed the sensitive muscles of her lower back. Her face was buried against her knees so that she was unaware of movement until she felt a pair of hands on her back. Then she jumped in alarm.

"No," he gently pushed her down again, "Hold still. Let me see if I can do something about that stiffness."

"How did you know it was stiff?" she asked, but her voice was muffled against her running suit.

"That little move a second ago. You stretched pretty gingerly." Homing in on precisely the spot, his thumbs began a circular kneading that brought a helpless moan of relief from Abby. "Feel better?"

"Does it ever!" she exhaled slowly.

"Does your back always bother you when you run?"

"Uh-uh. . . . Only when I stop."

"Very funny."

Abby might have laughed had it not been for her growing awareness of his fingers—not only those thumbs that pressed and rubbed, but the others, four on each side, that seemed to round her middle and stake their claim. There was nothing laughable about their strength, nor about their exquisite gentleness. And her eyes were no longer shut, but rather wide, wide open.

Suddenly Ben leaned forward. "I think that's about as much as I can take," he mused on a husky note. When she turned her head instinctively, she found his within inches. And his message couldn't have been more clearly broadcast than it was in the smooth quicksilver of his eyes, the manly lure of his mouth, the absolute earthiness about him.

Abby's heart pounded loudly with her acknowledgment that Ben Wyeth was not only good looking and companionable, but the sexiest man she'd seen in years. She felt the animal magnetism that radiated from him, felt it in the tingling response of her body.

They straightened slowly as a pair, neither breaking the silent spell. She took in his rumpled hair, his sweaty brow, the night's shadow of his beard and felt all the more attracted. Then her gaze fell to his lips and she watched them move.

"We'd better go in," he murmured.

She nodded mutely but couldn't budge.

"Abby . . ."

Eyes widened, she met his gaze, knowing only that she wanted him to kiss her. But his tone had been of warning and he clamped his mouth shut, daring only to stroke her cheek with the back of his hand before pushing himself to his feet.

Then he cleared his throat. "I think we ought to get showered and dressed," he said, offering her a hand up. "They say breakfast is set for seven-forty-five. We're supposed to be at the courthouse an hour after that."

Where better judgment hadn't had a chance, mention of the courthouse brought her to her senses. The trial . . . she'd nearly forgotten why she was here, why *he* was here. With a soft moan of self-reproach and an apprehensive wince, she walked, head down, through the door he held and moved distractedly toward the stairs.

The trial . . . beginning in just about two hours. Her stomach fluttered in a totally different way than it had moments before. As she headed up the first flight, she wondered what it would be like to sit there in the courtroom and not only watch the proceedings but be a vital participant in them.

It was only when she'd reached the landing of the

second floor that she realized Ben was still beside her. "I'll . . . I'll see you at breakfast," she half-whispered then turned to mount the flight to the third floor. Her footsteps were echoed the entire way. At the top it was Ben's turn.

"See you later," he murmured, waiting for her to turn left to his right. When she turned right as well, he stood stock still and watched her go.

Her hand was on her doorknob before she looked back at him. When she frowned and tipped her head in puzzlement, he advanced. He stopped no more than an arm's length away—an arm's length from Abby, an arm's length from his own door.

Suddenly his expression warmed with that same humor she'd found so appealing from the start. "This may prove to be as much of a trial as the other," he drawled, staring at her a minute longer before letting himself in and shutting the door.

Abby knew exactly what he meant.

three

HER PULSE QUICKENED. IT WAS ONE THING TO know that Ben's room was right next to hers, that each time she dressed or showered or climbed into bed he'd be doing the same little more than a wall's width away. But to arrive in court and find that they'd be seated beside one another throughout the long trial process was something else. It, too, was the luck of the draw—her twelfth to his thirteenth—and she had mixed feelings as to its merit.

There was, on the one hand, a certain solace at having him so close. While her own stomach knotted in anticipation of the start of the proceedings, he sat calmly, quietly, exuding a tranquility that gave her strength.

On the other hand, though, there was the way he looked, all clean and fresh and startlingly vibrant. His shirt was crisp and white, his blazer a dignified navy, his slacks . . . his slacks . . . she knew them to be gray, though her eye was more entranced by the way they spanned his thigh as he crossed one knee over the other.

All things considered, Abby wondered whether her stomach fluttered in response to the air of expectation in the courtroom . . . or in response to the stimulus of one thoroughly virile Benjamin Wyeth.

"Everything okay, Abby?" he asked softly. "You look a little peaked. We didn't wear you out this morning, did we?" The last was on a gently teasing note.

"Not on your life," she countered, quickly rising to his bait with the shadow of a smile. "I'm impressed that you guys kept up as well as you did." Then she glanced toward the crowd in the courtroom and her smile vanished. "It's this whole thing, I guess," she offered in explanation of her pallor. "I just wish we'd begin. It doesn't look like there's a free seat here."

Ben joined her in scanning the packed courtroom. "Only the defendant's. They must be waiting—ah, here he comes now."

A hush settled over the crowd as a door at the front of the courtroom opened and the defendant emerged accompanied by two guards, both uniformed, both alert. Abby noted that Derek Bradley was impeccably dressed, conservative in a dark gray three-piece suit and dark cordovans. He was freshly shaven, well groomed, and good looking. When he offered a fleeting smile toward the front row, where members of his family sat grouped together, Abby could see how many a woman might be charmed.

"I'm surprised the prosecution didn't challenge your selection," Ben leaned sideways to whisper. "Derek Bradley is young and attractive. And if he smiles at *you* that way . . ."

"Don't be absurd," she came back with a forceful whisper of her own. "He's not *that* good looking. Besides, he can't be a day over thirty. I like my men older . . . more mellow."

He arched a brow. "That's encouraging. Maybe the prosecution knew what it was doing after all. Either that . . . or they ran out of challenges." His eyes were warm as they studied her, and Abby felt her cheeks flush in response. But she was saved from the need to answer him by the loud rap of a gavel to her left.

"Please rise in honor of the court," the clerk of court intoned loudly. Every soul in the courtroom stood.

Abby gripped the wooden railing that separated the two rows of jurors and watched wide-eyed as the judges appeared at a door to her right. Single file, with black-robed Theodore Hammond in the middle, the three slowly mounted the bench.

"Be seated," the clerk directed. Every soul in the courtroom sat.

Abby was only too glad to be off her feet again. Her knees had been none too steady, her palms none too dry . . . and Benjamin Wyeth had been far too tall and straight by her side to ignore. At least now the arms of the brown leather chairs separated them.

Glancing down, she was caught by the contrast of her creamy silk sleeve against his of navy wool, her slimness against his muscled strength. A wave of primal sensitivity surged through her. So much for the saving grace of brown leather chairs, she mused in dismay as she diplomatically tucked in her elbows, folded her hands in her lap, and did her best to turn her attention to the court.

The crowd stilled when the clerk stood to read the indictments, naming the defendant, Derek Bradley, on charges of kidnapping and assault and battery. At the arraignment months before, pleas of not guilty had been entered. Now the words reechoed through the courtroom.

Then, as Grace had warned, the judge took several minutes to address the jury. "Ladies and gentlemen," he began gravely, "you've been asked to make a sacrifice that many of your fellow citizens have never and will never be asked to make. For the sake of justice, you have agreed to surrender your freedom for the duration of this trial. The court recognizes the extent of this sacrifice and hereby thanks you on behalf of the state of Vermont."

Abby hung on his every word, as did each of her fellow jurors. Not one moved. Not one acknowledged the fact that the eyes of the courtroom were upon them.

"As this trial progresses, you will be presented with arguments and evidence by representatives of two opposing sides. We ask that you listen carefully to each and every point, since it will be your job to make a final decision as to the guilt or innocence of the defendant."

He paused to frown at the papers on his desk before continuing. "As you know, the purpose of sequestration is to prevent your being influenced, one way or the other, by outside forces. The only sources of input you're to have regarding this case are myself and my side judges, the prosecution team and its witnesses, and the defense team and its witnesses. You are neither to hear anything about this case from nor discuss anything about this case with any other person.

"Unfortunately, that includes each other. Difficult as it may be, I ask that you don't discuss this case among yourselves. When the time comes for deliberations, you will be able to do so—but only *after* each side has rested its case.

"If you have questions or problems of any sort, the court officers are at your service. Wherever possible they'll try to minimize the inconvenience that this experience must be for you. Feel free to ask their help." Looking first to one side then the other, the judge silently asked his partners on the bench if they had anything to add. When two headshakes had been received, he nodded and turned to the prosecution table. "Mr. Weitz?"

The opening argument of the state's attorney lasted for nearly an hour. It was offered in the low-key style that would come to be associated with David Weitz, but was as emotion-packed in content as its presentation was straight.

The prosecutor began with the premise that Derek Bradley, in a cool and premeditated act, had kidnapped his former lover, Greta Robinson, with the intent of punishing her for spurning him and forcing a return of her affections. He went on to paint the defendant as a self-centered man, a man of inherited wealth, who had come to believe that his power was boundless, that his will was the law. He cited witnesses who would testify not only to the facts of the case but to Derek Bradley's arrogance, his selfishness, his tyrannical personality. And he suggested that, after days of emotional torture in an isolated cabin, Greta Robinson was scarred for life.

When he'd concluded his opening presentation, the judge called a fifteen-minute recess and disappeared with his colleagues into their chambers. The jury was led down to the first-floor jury room, where coffee and doughnuts were served.

Abby took a chair by herself, deep in thought, neither terribly thirsty nor particularly hungry. She was amazed at how simple he'd made Bradley's action sound, how clear-cut, how wrong. Had a vote been held at that very minute she would surely have found Derek Bradley guilty. But there was still another side to hear, she told herself, and this was just the *opening* argument.

"I can't get you any coffee?" Ben asked, bending over her chair, his hand on its back.

Startled from her thoughts, she looked up quickly. "Coffee? Uh . . . no, no, thanks."

"It's good coffee." He tried temptation as he settled down beside her. Leaning forward with his elbows propped on his thighs, he balanced his own cup between his palms.

Abby smiled begrudgingly. "I think I've got enough adrenaline surging through these veins to forgo the caffeine. It's not good for you, you know . . . caffeine. Does a job on the pancreas . . . among other things."

Ben shot her a glance as he took a deliberate sip from his cup. "So they tell me," he murmured in amusement. "Is the nurse a crusader?"

"This is the woman speaking . . . and I'm certainly no crusader." She gave a pert shrug. "Feel free to drink whatever you want." Then she paused to watch him swirl the cup, lift it to his lips, scowl, and lower it again without so much as a sip, and she stifled a smug grin. "I'll bet you down plenty of that stuff when you're working to finish a manuscript."

His gaze was enigmatic. "A manuscript?"

She rubbed her forehead with her fingers. "I keep coming up with China . . . was that it?"

". . . It was."

Hearing the hesitation in his voice, Abby eyed him quizzically. "You seem disturbed. Is something wrong?"

"No. . . . Not really. I'm just . . . surprised. That book wasn't exactly a best seller."

"Andre seemed to think it was great."

"Who's Andre?"

"A friend."

"A *fiancé* type of friend?" he asked, a bit of the old humor returning.

Abby couldn't help but chuckle. "No. A friend type of friend. He owns a bookstore, and I happened to be around when your books first arrived. I got the impression that they sold well."

"China's an 'in' topic." He shrugged. But he'd straightened in his seat and was far from nonchalant.

"Don't tell me your book is a travelogue," she teased.

"No." He seemed hesitant to discuss it though, somehow uncomfortable.

"Well . . ." she prodded softly, allowing curiosity to get the better of her.

Overcoming reticence, he spoke at last. "It's an analysis of transitional politics in the People's Republic. China has fascinated me for years. When the opportunity to visit it finally came up, I knew that I'd have to write the book." It was as though he were excusing himself. Abby couldn't understand it.

"That's great, Ben. You must be proud of the book. Was it your first?"

"First significant one . . . yes."

"Have you written others since?"

"One other."

Her eyes lit up. "Finished?"

"Uh-huh."

There was something that wasn't being said. She could see it in the depths of his eyes, feel it in his quiet intensity. While she waited expectantly, he sat perfectly still.

Suddenly the wheels of her mind fell into gear and began to turn. Yesterday morning, here in this same jury room, they'd shared something none of the others had felt. It had been a mutually favorable bent toward serving on this jury. Abby knew *her* reasons for welcoming the experience. As of this morning, Ben knew them too.

But as yet the tables hadn't been turned. She was still in the dark as to *his* motives. Now . . . to learn he was a writer . . . She stared at him with growing awareness. Could he . . . would he . . .

At that moment, the break was declared over, and the jurors stood to file back upstairs. "Ben . . . ?"

A long forefinger touched his lips as he signaled her to silence. "Later," he murmured, guiding her before him, out into the hall toward the stairs. Hopelessly immersed amid the others, Abby had to be satisfied with the quiet promise.

Back in the courtroom, David Weitz put on his first witness, a woman who testified to having seen the abduction. It had been dusk. She'd been driving home from work when she'd seen a man step smoothly from his parked car and grab the arm of a passing woman. There had been an argument, then a tussle. The man had finally pulled the woman around the car to the driver's side and had forced her in before slipping in himself and driving off.

On direct examination, the witness identified photographs of the victim, Greta Robinson. She also described the assailant as a man of the same height, weight, and build as Derek Bradley but could go no further toward a positive identification since the man she'd observed had been wearing a wool hat and tinted glasses and his parka collar had been pulled to his ears. She admitted to having shrugged off the incident as a domestic feud . . . until she'd seen photographs of the missing woman in the newspaper several days later.

Abby listened intently to the testimony. One question at a time was asked of the witness, only the simplest answer was allowed. It was a slow and painstaking process, but the state's attorney was determined to do it right.

Under cross-examination by defense counsel, the witness was treated less kindly. Was she *sure* there had been an argument? How could she tell, if her car was several lengths away and her windows rolled up against the February chill? Did she actually hear anything? Did the alleged victim *struggle* as she was being led to the driver's side of the car? What did this struggle entail? It had been dusk; could she be sure that she'd identified the victim correctly? And the defendant—how could she discern his build through his parka? What color had his parka been? Could she be sure that it was Derek Bradley she'd seen? Could she be *absolutely* sure?

The tone of the session had risen in pitch with the defense's cross-examination. If David Weitz was generally soft-spoken, William Montgomery was his fiery counterpart. By the time the witness had been dismissed and the court recessed for lunch, Abby had had a taste of the challenge she and her fellow jurors faced.

As she'd only suspected earlier, facts that seemed crystal clear one minute were easily clouded the next with the introduction of a second side, a second point of view. Despite oaths to tell "the whole truth and nothing but," there were any number of different perceptions and interpretations of the truth. This was what the jurors would have to wade through before their own ordeal was over.

If Abby had hoped to gain courage from Ben during the ninety-minute lunch break, she was to be disappointed. For he was somehow separated from her during the walk downstairs, and she found herself eating lunch with Patsy and Louise.

All three were subdued, as indeed were the others. With the morning's testimony fresh in their minds, there was much to consider, little to discuss. The meal was brought in to the jury room and was a soup-and-sandwich-to-go affair that would set precedent for the days ahead. The room itself—the same one in which Abby had sat yesterday, the same one to which the jury had been brought first thing this morning, the same one in which their break had been held earlier—was T-shaped, with straight wooden chairs, side to side, lining every wall, and a large central table on which the food was set.

"Thank heavens the chairs upstairs are more comfortable," Patsy murmured as she tried to balance her lunch on her lap while squirming to get comfortable.

Abby grimaced. "I'll second that. But it looks like we'll be spending plenty of time down here too."

"Do they always take so many breaks?"

Louise leaned forward, her voice a whisper. "They wouldn't want us to go hungry, would they? After all, the show's being put on for our benefit."

Relieved that there seemed no bitterness in Louise's quip, Abby smiled. "I hadn't thought of it quite that way before, but you've got a point. When it comes right down to it, each lawyer will try to do his best to sway us to his way of thinking."

"And the facts?" Louise interjected more grimly. "Shouldn't they be able to speak for themselves?"

"I'm sure they do sometimes," Abby reasoned aloud. "Still . . . when the facts are hazy . . ." Her voice trailed off as she verged on the forbidden. The others understood.

"Hmmmph," Patsy grunted, but good-naturedly this time, "I'd cast my vote for whoever can do something about these chairs."

Abby smiled. "It's because you're so slim, Patsy," she teased. "Now if you had a little more padding in certain spots . . ."

"Look who's talking," the blonde quipped.

"You're *both* crazy," Louise said as she took a large bite of her sandwich, but Abby was sure she'd seen the beginnings of a smile, and she was satisfied.

Between bits and snatches of light conversation,

she found herself relaxing more. By the time she'd finished eating, the morning's events seemed safely put in perspective. Unfortunately, though, with this gradual release came a renewed awareness of Ben, who sat at the far end of the room, engrossed in quiet discussion with one of the other men.

There were so many questions she suddenly wanted to ask—about his work, his travels, his aspirations. What was it that drew them together? Sheer diversion? The buds of true friendship? Or . . . or . . . was it that same something that made her tremble as she recalled how he'd been that morning, all tousled and sweaty and breathtakingly masculine.

When she could take no more of her self-induced torment, she stood and turned her back to stare out the window. The leaves had already begun to turn and would be reaching their peak during the next few weeks. Autumn had always been one of her favorite seasons, a time for coming in and bundling up and setting the first of the logs ablaze in the fireplace. Even now, she could smell the fragrance of dry birch and pine. There was nothing more romantic. . . .

"Penny for your thoughts."

Abby looked quickly up at Ben's warm features, then returned to the less dangerous sight of the green beyond the courthouse. "I was just thinking about fall. It's a beautiful season."

"That it is. Football . . . chestnuts . . . the smell of burning leaves." He inhaled deeply. "I don't know, though. It smells different this year. Sweeter . . . more sophisticated."

Abby gave him a gentle nudge in the ribs. "That's my perfume," she chided, but caught her breath when she felt his lips by her ear.

"I was wondering what was driving me crazy all morning. You did it on purpose, didn't you?"

"Who . . . me? But I always wear it. . . ."

"Then I'm in big trouble." He lengthened the "big" for emphasis.

She shrugged. "You seemed to find the perfect solution just now. All you have to do is to stay on the far side of the room."

"You missed me," he said softly, and she knew she had to do something to redirect his thoughts.

"Actually," she began, turning to lean back on the window sill and face him, "I was looking forward to hearing about this book you're going to write."

"Which one?"

At his look of utter innocence, she sighed. ". . . The one about the jury process."

"Aaaaaaah . . . *that* one."

She waited, but he said nothing more. "Come on, Ben. That *is* one of the side benefits to serving on this jury, isn't it?"

He raised a speculative brow, then let it fall. "Perhaps."

"You mean to say you haven't already begun to do research? Wasn't that what mixing last night at dinner was about . . . and lunch just now?"

A spark of silver flashed in his eyes. "You did miss me. I think you're jealous." He seemed eminently pleased at the possibility.

"Jealous?" she asked, swallowing hard. "Not on your life," she lied. "I'd just like to know what's for the sake of research . . . and what's for real." Until she'd said it, she hadn't quite thought of it that way. But it was the truth. There was a tiny part of her that feared *she* was part of his study, and the thought hurt.

Ben's eyes held hers, reading her emotions. When he raised his hand to her cheek, his touch held only tenderness. Again she felt it . . . that same something that surged between them each time they were together. She could almost forget where they were, that there were others around, that they'd soon be returning to the courtroom. She could almost forget . . . almost . . . but not quite.

"Ben . . . Abby?" Grace broke into their mindlock as gently as possible. "They'd like us back upstairs now."

Slowly dropping his hand, Ben took a deep breath and straightened. "Later, Abby, later," he murmured as he stood back to let her pass.

Abby pondered his words as she lay on her bed late that afternoon. Later. When would *that* be? And what would happen then? More critically, what did she *want* to happen?

But just as courtroom issues were shady at points, so the question she asked herself had no easy answer. On the one hand, she wanted Ben to tell her of his thoughts, to reassure her that the spark between them was real, to kiss her and hold her in proof of its existence. On the other hand, she wanted him to say nothing further, to be as detached and self-contained as the other jurors appeared to be. For one fact simply couldn't be denied. She and Ben were members of a jury impaneled to make an important decision in the days ahead. The thought of a love affair in the process was preposterous.

It was a war between emotion and reason with no truce in sight. Shifting restlessly, she looked toward the wall . . . his wall. What was he doing now, thinking, wearing? Would he really write a book on his experience as a juror? And who had he spoken to last night on the phone just before she'd received her call from Sean?

Bolting upright in self-reproach, she threw herself into the chair, snatched up a notebook and pen, and began to record what had happened in court that day. It was something she'd decided to do when she'd first been impaneled, something she felt might make the restriction the judge had imposed on discussion of the trial easier to bear. True, it was a personal outlet of sorts. But having passed a full day in court, she saw another benefit. Given the abundance of details introduced into evidence, her notes might well be of help to her when the time for deliberations arrived.

Writing quickly, she recreated the events of the morning, then moved on. The afternoon's session had commanded concentration as intense as had the morning session. This time, the witness had been the police officer who had tracked down and finally rescued Greta Robinson. The testimony had been tedious, laced with dates and times and locations. There had been a missing person's report and a subsequent search, then the appearance of the witness who claimed to have seen the abduction. There had been lead upon lead, one falling flat on the next, until a pair of hikers had returned from a wooded area far north with reports of a locked cabin . . . and a woman's cry from within.

A soft knock on the door made her jump. Catching her breath, she laid her pen and paper on the table and went to answer it. On the other side stood Ben, wearing a plaid shirt, jeans, and sneakers, looking handsome enough to shake her breathing all the more.

"You weren't sleeping?" he asked by way of apology, only then taking in her own sweater and jeans.

"No, no," she offered with a wave toward the table. "I was just making some notes for myself . . . but I could used the break. Things get very dramatic, even in hindsight."

"I know what you mean." He hesitated. "How about a walk?"

Was this the "later" he'd promised? "Can we?" she asked, her eyes alight. "I mean, are we allowed out, uh, on our own?" For some reason she felt foolishly young just then. She couldn't decide whether it was the need to get permission to go out . . . or her giddiness at the thought of going out with Ben.

"I've checked with the desk, and they say we're allowed to walk by ourselves . . . as long as we stay within sight of the inn."

Both recalled the morning's run, when they'd ventured much farther than that. Ray had been with them then. Now, though, neither of them particularly wanted his company.

"Sounds fine." She turned toward the closet. "Just let me get something for my feet." Kneeling, she retrieved her sneakers and sank into the chair to put them on.

Ben had stepped forward to lean against the doorjamb. "Your room's very much like mine," he observed as his eye skirted it. "Different colors perhaps, different artwork . . . and of course," he pushed himself from the jamb and walked toward the dresser, "there isn't a bottle of perfume in sight."

Abby watched as he lifted the decorative bottle, unscrewed its cap, and inhaled deeply. Then, as deliberately, he set it down and turned to her, his mien suddenly more alert, his features tauter. His eyes told the story though, warm to the point of smoldering.

At a strange loss for words, she snapped back to tying her laces. When her fingers stumbled, she had to start again; the simple process seemed to take forever. When she straightened, Ben was directly before her.

"Don't look at me that way," she half-teased, but her voice was shaky. *"I* didn't tell you to walk in and smell the stuff."

"But you're sitting there so damned appealing . . ." he said in a tone that held its share of accusation. Reaching down, he drew her up. She couldn't have thought to resist the gentle strength of his arms. It seemed that she'd wanted him to touch her all along.

Her eyes met his, and once more she felt that same silent force. She tried to remind herself of the time and place, that they were two people thrown together for an intensive three-week trial. But nothing could cool the heat she felt radiating from him, into her, and back.

Slowly he lifted his hands to frame her face. His fingers wove into her hair, savoring its dark luxuriance. His thumbs lightly explored her lips before falling back to clear the way. Abby heard the catch in his breath, felt its warmth against her mouth. Yet he held back, not quite kissing her, sampling the excitement to be gained from the waiting.

She'd never known such sweet anticipation. It was as though they had all the time in the world to enjoy the small pleasures of life. Perhaps it was the situation; perhaps the thought of pain between man and woman, the trial's main concern, had given them a greater appreciation of something each had taken for granted before. She didn't know for sure. But she surrendered to the pure delight she felt as he grazed her cheeks, her chin, the tip of her nose. It was only when her lips parted in warm invitation that he finally gave in to his own ardent need.

His kiss was full and rich, as heady as any wine she'd ever drunk. It seemed to consume her, to draw her into him just as his gaze could always do. Weak in the knees, Abby clung to him, unaware that she'd touched him until her arms met each other at the nape of his neck. She moaned against his mouth when she felt him complete the embrace.

"Oh, Abby . . . Abby . . ." Tearing his lips from hers, he crushed her against him. "Why here . . . why now?" he rasped against her hair.

But she had no answer to the anguish in his voice, nor did she fully understand it. And she was too overwhelmed by her own emotions to do much more than tremble silently against him.

Gradually the ragged tempo of his heartbeat eased, and she felt his tautness relax. Only then was she able to look up at him. "What happened to that walk?" she whispered hoarsely, her own pulse still erratic.

Ben cleared his throat. "Good thinking. . . . That walk." In a deliberate motion he set her back, then raked his hands through his hair, looked down at the rug and frowned. "Look, Abby—"

"No, Ben," she began, holding up a hand for his silence. "Please don't say anything." Some tiny part of her wasn't sure she wanted his apology. That would imply he was sorry he'd kissed her . . . and *she* wasn't.

But he was determined. His fingers grasped her shoulders with a strange fierceness. "That shouldn't have happened. Not with what we've got ahead of us. But, damn it, I've wanted to kiss you since I first saw you yesterday!"

Stunned by his begrudging admission and the force behind it, she stared mutely up at him. Then she realized the truth of his words. His was the voice of reason, the small voice she'd ignored within herself. He was right; their timing *was* wrong. But, Lord help her, she wanted him to kiss her again.

"Look," he growled, "maybe we'd better forget that walk."

"No!" she exclaimed, then managed to lower her voice. "I do need a break. Fresh air. Something. If I sit here until dinner, I'll only rehash the day in court, and I've got to get away from it. . . ." It was only half the truth. If she sat there alone now, she'd also rehash the feelings she'd experienced in Ben's arms. But he didn't want to hear *that.*

Dropping his hands from her shoulders, he stepped back. Then he rubbed the muscles at the back of his neck. "You're not the only one. . . . Okay. Let's go."

They walked in silence down two flights of stairs, through the large foyer, and out. Though the sun's shadows were lengthening by the minute, the day was far from gone. Abby stood for a minute in the path of one golden streak, turned her face to its source, and breathed in deeply. It felt good to be outside; she should have done this the minute she'd returned. The air was invigorating, the sun's rays warm. Relaxation was fully within her grasp.

"Abby . . ."

Opening her eyes, she saw Ben staring at her. "Sorry," she murmured and trotted down the last step. Then, following his lead, she matched her stride to his. With the crisp grass of autumn whispering beneath their shoes, they slowly made a broad circle around the inn, finally coming to rest side by side against the base of an ancient oak. It was Ben who spoke first.

"What were you writing when I interrupted you?" he asked, leaning back against the ridged bark and gazing lazily toward the leaves above.

She pulled at a blade of grass and fingered it idly. "I was writing down what went on today. You know, witnesses and facts and dates and all. This was only the first day, and there's so much to remember.

What's going to happen after ten or twelve days of testimony?"

He chuckled. "We'll either be very confused . . . or totally convinced."

"I suppose you're right," she mused. "But still, I feel better making notes at the end of each day. And since we can't discuss the case with anyone, I suppose it's like a diary."

"You sound like *you* should be the one writing a book. . . ."

She looked up to find him watching her closely. "Tell me about it, Ben. I think it's a fascinating idea."

"*You* may think so, but I'm not sure the others would agree if they knew what I was doing."

She recalled her comment about differentiating between research and reality. "They don't have to know now, do they?"

For the first time since he'd arrived at her room, Ben smiled. "Then I can count on you to keep my secret?"

"Of course, you can." She turned to face him head on. "Did you really think I'd tell them to watch their words when you're around?" She laughed softly. "I'm more curious to see if you can get them to open up . . . even *without* their knowing your ulterior motive."

"Oh, I'll get them talking."

"You seem very sure."

"It's the circumstances, Abby. There's an initial wariness they feel toward each other, toward the trial itself. As time goes on, they'll open up . . . to satisfy a very basic human need, if nothing else."

She reflected for a minute on the basic human need *she* felt and frowned in puzzlement. It was a basic *feminine* need, where Ben was concerned. But why now? Why here? Then she caught her breath as she realized she'd echoed the questions he'd asked earlier.

"Tell me about yourself, Abby," he asked now.

He'd caught her at the moment she was vulnerable, when the door to her soul had been open. Looking away to hide her confusion, she shrugged. "What would you like to know?"

"How long have you lived here?"

"Three years. I moved up from New York."

"Ah . . . the big city." Bourbon and water.

"That's right."

"What were you doing there?"

"I worked in the pediatric ward of a hospital."

"You must love children."

"Yes."

"But you don't have your own."

"Nope."

"Aside from not having married, any other reason?"

Resting her head back against the tree, she grew more reflective. "I've got time. I'm just not ready . . . for either marriage *or* children. When the time's right, I'll know it."

"What about your fiancé?"

She shot him a fast glance. "He's *not* my fiancé."

"Then . . . what? You must have *some* sort of relationship with him—for him to call on the phone and announce himself that way."

"He's my boss."

"Your *boss?* You're carrying on an affair with your *boss?*"

"Not . . . quite," she drawled. Then she studied his dark expression and grinned. "If I didn't know better I'd say *you* were jealous."

"Damned right I am," he admitted without hesitation. "You're a beautiful woman, Abby."

As his tone grew more husky, she felt her own response. But before it could swell to anything more than a gentle tremor in her limbs, she wrenched her gaze from his and looked off toward the garden house. It seemed unfair that Ben should be able to excite her with no more than a word, a tone, a glance. She'd never felt this deep stirring for Sean. Had she *ever* felt it before? Or had the fact of sequestration, a kind of contrived captivity in itself, done something to her senses?

"You never told me how the college is managing without you for these three weeks," she said, drawing on one of the many questions in her mind in an attempt to bank the fire. "Hasn't the semester just begun?"

Ben indulged her momentarily. "Jury duty is high-priority stuff. My colleagues will cover for me."

"Particularly if a book is forthcoming from the experience?"

He didn't answer, simply studied her. Then his indulgence ended. "Why would your . . . your boss call himself your fiancé?"

"Uh-oh. We're back to that again?"

"Why not? I have an interesting theory." He looked toward the horizon and gestured where headlines might be. "Beautiful young nurse chased around examining room by doctor madly and passionately in love with her."

"That's absurd, Ben! Sean doesn't *chase* me." Not in the most ludicrous sense, at least.

"Do you date him?"

"Yes. . . . He's a nice guy."

"A 'nice guy'? Hmmmmm. That's a poison for passion if there ever was one." He paused. "But . . . is it true?"

"Is what true?"

"That he's in love with you?"

She shrugged. "He says he is."

"And you're stringing him along?"

Abby looked up sharply. "I wouldn't say that. I've told him over and over again that I'm not in love with him and that I won't marry him. I don't exactly call that 'stringing him along.' "

"But the poor guy may be suffering. . . ."

"That's not *my* fault!" she exclaimed with growing indignation. "How much more blunt can I be? Or do you suggest that I agree to marry him"—she snapped her fingers—"just like that?"

Unfazed by her show of irritation, Ben delved further. "He's a doctor, isn't he? You could do worse," he stated with a calmness that irked her all the more.

Abby's spine stiffened. "I don't believe you, Ben! You sound like my mother!"

"Maybe she has a point."

"She's not the one being pushed into marriage. If I don't love Sean, I won't marry him. My Lord, the divorce rate is high enough!"

"But surely there would be *something* in it for you . . . even without love. Security . . . kids . . . sex . . . ?"

Fully incensed now, she scrambled to her feet and stood before him with her hands on her hips. "It so happens that I *have* security. I have a good job . . . and a trust fund left by my father. Furthermore," she gulped, "I have kids . . . dozens and dozens of them, all of whom I can send home at the end of the day. And as for sex . . ." she raged, "as for sex . . . Sean Hennessy just doesn't turn me on. Besides," she added on a note of spite, "these are modern times. If a woman needs a bedmate, she takes one . . . with or without a wedding band!"

Her hair flew out behind as she whirled on her heel and headed for the inn. Her blood pounded in her ears, her chest heaved. She'd never been as irate in her life. Irate . . . hurt . . . disappointed.

Storming up the front steps, she was filled with dismay that Ben could have said what he had. Security...kids...sex...bah! Typically masculine point of view. No love . . . never love. Was it exclusively a woman's emotion?

True, Sean believed he loved her. . . . But he, too, seemed to feel that a marriage could survive without that one element. And what had his love consisted of? He said she was bright, hard-working, and wonderful with kids. The perfect little wife and mother, she fumed as she slammed through the front door and attacked the stairs at a jogger's pace.

But Sean had never pushed her physically. Now she wondered why. Oh, he'd kissed her and crooned sexy thoughts to her. They'd even indulged in a little petting. But when Abby pulled back, he never complained. Did he too feel that something was missing? Was he reluctant finally to accept the fact that the chemistry was all wrong?

Rounding one flight and loping up the next, she reran Ben's words. Security . . . she had it. Kids . . . perhaps there *was* more to the issue there. It was one thing to find pleasure in other people's children, quite another to experience the joy of one's own. She wasn't blind to her deep maternal instincts, nor did she doubt that one day she *would* want a child. But motherhood was no reason to rush into marriage with Sean . . . particularly when something deep within told her she could have it all. . . .

And sex. The big S. First and foremost on every man's mind. With an angry scowl and a low-muttered oath, she slammed the door of her room and leaned back against it. There, too, she'd only told half the story. Modern women *were* freer than ever in satisfying their own desires. And she hadn't reached the age of twenty-eight a virgin. But she de-

manded something beyond the purely physical,
something to give meaning to those joys of the flesh.
Not marriage, nor promises, she mused, but love.
Very simply. Love.

four

BEN GAVE ABBY TIME TO LICK HER WOUNDS. He saw her at meals, ran with her in the morning, sat beside her in court. But other than a cordial greeting or a brief passing remark, he made no attempt to seek her out personally as he'd done that Thursday night.

It wasn't that Abby wanted an apology. When she thought about it, Ben had done no more than probe her feelings about marriage in general, and Sean in particular. And he hadn't actually said that *he* believed in marriage without love, had he?

With the passage of time her anger eased, and she became more concerned with why it had arisen in the first place. When it came to Ben Wyeth, she reflected, everything *about* her seemed to react strongly. Even now, despite the subtle barrier between them, she felt his presence every time he came near.

In a way she was grateful for the trial, which demanded her complete concentration. During those hours, and the periods of slow unwinding immediately after, she was preoccupied, thinking neither of Sean, nor her patients, nor her house, her mail, her friends . . . nor Ben. As fate would have it though, Ben was always the first to reenter her thoughts.

The blame rested, she told herself, on the nature of their bizarre adventure. To be locked away from the rest of the world, with thirteen strangers, several guards, and a handful of inn personnel . . . it *was* unusual. Under the circumstances, it would be perfectly normal for a woman like her to be drawn to a man like Ben. When the trial was over and they were all back in the "real world" . . . that would be something else. She'd go her way, back to her job, her kids, and Sean; he'd go his way, back to the college, his books, and . . . and . . . who *was* that he spoke with on the phone each night? A colleague? A friend? A . . . a . . . lover? This was the thought that disturbed her most, and regardless of how she tried, she couldn't shake a feeling of jealousy.

Annoyed at that and determined to overcome it, she made a concerted effort to get to know the other jurors. Several remained aloof. Several others had formed their own small clique. Several, though, she found to be truly companionable once they'd settled into the routine.

And Patsy continued to be a pleasure. She and Abby grew closer. "Abby?" She knocked softly on the door before breakfast on Saturday morning. "Abby . . . it's Patsy. Are you up?"

"Coming," came the muffled cry as Abby emerged from the bathroom in her slip, towel-drying her hair as she went for the door. "Hi," she said, stepping back to let Patsy in, then shutting the door behind her. "I'm almost ready." She'd run earlier with the others and had just showered and put on a light sheen of makeup. "What's up?"

"Have you heard where we're going?" Patsy asked, eyes filled with excitement.

"I thought we were going to court," Abby said, as

she vigorously rubbed her hair with the towel. The judge had declared that morning sessions would be held on Saturdays in hopes of thereby ending the trial a day or two earlier.

"We are. But *after*. This afternoon."

Abby's hand stopped mid-air, her eyes widening in interest. "They're taking us out?"

Patsy nodded eagerly. "We're going up to some hunting lodge near Stockbridge. It's supposed to be really nice. There's a lake there for swimming and canoeing, beautiful grounds, and I think they're planning a barbecue."

"Sounds like fun." She resumed her toweling. "I hadn't realized we'd be entertained in the off-hours like that."

"John said we'll be going out more as the trial goes on." John was the court officer who'd originally taken Abby from the courthouse to the inn. Between Ray, Grace, Lorraine, and John, the jurors were covered at all times. "He mentioned the movies and different restaurants. They may even take us mountain climbing."

"Now that *does* sound good. I've never climbed a real mountain before. But it's got to be an awful chore for the sheriff," Abby mused, dropping the towel to the bed and stepping into her skirt. "He has to clear every place we go. All it takes is one crackpot yelling 'Hang Bradley!' "—she'd cupped her mouth and distorted her voice, then returned it to normal—"and the judge'd get very nervous."

Patsy laughed gaily. "That's ridiculous. I think we know better than to listen to one fanatic."

"I hope so," Abby agreed, buttoning her blouse. They both knew though that it wasn't the occasional loud-mouth that frightened the judge. It was the fact that Derek Bradley's father was a prominent and wealthy member of the Burlington community, that he had major banking interests throughout the state, that he also owned large chunks of newspapers in both Rutland and Montpelier. Any juror on the panel would be easy prey for an imaginative blackmailer.

Patsy's spirits were dampened briefly. "What *would* happen if someone did that—you know, jumped in front of us and started yelling things."

"I assume that Ray and John would have him wrestled to the ground and muzzled before he knew what hit him."

"No . . . I mean, would there be an automatic mistrial declared?"

"I suppose that would depend on the situation. If the judge felt that we weren't actually *influenced* by the person, that we didn't feel pressured to agree with him, he might let it go. Or if only one or two of us were affected, we might be dismissed. With fourteen of us impaneled, there'd still be the necessary twelve left to deliberate. The state's made a huge investment in this trial. A new trial would only cost thousands more."

Patsy remained pensive. "What if someone . . . harmless . . . got through the sheriff's guards?" She flicked her head to the side. "You know, a bystander accidentally walking among us . . . or something. Would there be any . . . problem then?"

Plugging in her blow-dryer, Abby turned it on and gently finger-combed the warm air through her hair. "I suppose that depends. If the breach in security were truly accidental, I'm sure the guards would let it go. They've got their investment in this thing, too."

Patsy nodded, but said nothing more. As Abby cast a glance through the mirror at the downcast blond head, she wondered whether her friend mightn't have had something further in mind. But the head bobbed up with renewed enthusiasm before she could probe.

"Did Sean call again last night?"

"Uh-huh."

"Anything new?"

Abby gave a good-natured grimace. "Oh, yes. He suggested he might talk me into a case of high blood pressure . . . so that I'd have to be dismissed from the jury and placed under a doctor's care. He's incorrigible!"

"That's very sweet, Abby. He misses you."

"Now . . . don't *you* start on me too!" Abby exclaimed without thinking.

Patsy grinned mischievously. "Who beat me to it?" Abby's silence tipped her off. "It was Ben, wasn't it? See, he likes you enough to be nervous about Sean."

"I wouldn't say he's *nervous,"* Abby came back quickly, "and it's got nothing to do with whether he likes me or not. He just . . . sympathizes with the man, that's all."

"How's it going with him?"

"With Ben?" At Patsy's nod, she switched off the dryer and turned to lean back against the dresser. "It's not. He is a very pleasant man who happens to be on this jury." It sounded so simple.

"He also 'happens' to sit beside you every day, to run with you every morning, and to have a room right next to yours." The complications began to mount.

"And how do you know all that?" Abby eyed her skeptically. To her knowledge, Patsy had neither seen them running nor followed them up the stairs on their return. Patsy's own room was at the far end of the second floor.

"Oh . . . I know," the blonde said with an impish shrug. "I also know that he's aware of you even when

you try to ignore him. Last night after dinner, when
you were playing chess with Brian . . . then later,
when we were watching television . . ." She caught
her breath as a new thought intruded. "It's really a
pain, isn't it . . . things being monitored like that.
Poor Ray . . . having to jump up at every commercial
and turn off the sound so we won't hear anything if
there's a newsbreak."

"That's all part of it," Abby mused. "Maybe we'll
get used to it after a while. . . ."

"But Ben had his eye on you, Abby." Patsy flipped
the channel of her mind back to her own ongoing
program. "He's very subtle about it . . . but *I* can tell.
He's really gorgeous, you know. If I didn't have my
own eyes set on one adorable ski bum . . ."

"How is he, by the way? Did *he* call?"

"Three times. Grace wasn't too thrilled last
night."

Relieved to have shifted the conversation from
Ben, Abby engaged a bright-eyed Patsy in discussion
of her persistent beau as the two walked down to
breakfast.

Unfortunately, though, the bug had been planted
in Abby's ear. She was all the more conscious of Ben
through breakfast and the morning in court, wondering as she looked straight ahead whether he was
looking at her, thinking of her. It didn't help that
there seemed more sidebar discussions than ever;
during those times, when both prosecutor and defender met quietly with the judges at the far side of
the bench, the jury had nothing to do but to sit, perhaps talk softly among themselves.

"You've heard about this afternoon, haven't
you?" Ben murmured during one of those idle times.

"Uh-huh. The hunting lodge."

"Have you got a bathing suit with you?"

"I've got one . . . but isn't it a little too cold?"

"Too cold," he grinned, "for an athlete like you?" His teasing caused her insides to shiver in a way that had nothing to do with the temperature.

"Running is one thing, swimming something else. When you run, you wear warm-ups and sneakers and a hat. When you swim, you wear practically nothing. . . . I mean," she stumbled in embarrassment and could have strangled herself there and then, "a bathing suit doesn't do much for warmth."

Ben didn't miss the flush on her cheeks. "True," he said calmly. His eyes were more intense. "But it might be okay this afternoon. Besides, if you swim long enough, you build up a sweat."

"You're kidding."

"Nope. Try it."

"Are you saying that you swim . . . in addition to running?"

"Sometimes."

In the silence that ensued, they looked at each other intently. Just then, Abby knew she'd missed him—missed his gentleness, his warm banter. . . . A stirring in the courtroom signaled the end of the bench conference; the judge's deep voice broke the spell.

Abby couldn't forget it though, as morning became history and they returned to the inn for lunch, then piled back into the vans to head north. Nor could she forget it when the drive took them on a tour of autumn in Vermont, and her mind filled with the same romantic thoughts Ben had once before evoked. He sat in the front seat talking with Ray; she sat in the third row behind. Still she could almost feel the thickness of his hair, the strength of the arm thrown across the back of the seat, the warmth of the lips that moved companionably. And she couldn't help but wonder whether he'd ever kiss her again.

Lost in a world of increasingly melancholy day-dreams, she sat quietly through most of the ride, as did Patsy, who sat beside her. Beautiful as the scenery was, both women were more than happy to alight from the van when it finally pulled up at its destination.

The hunting lodge was large and rugged. It was inviting in a down-home sort of way, a contrast both to the properly formal courthouse and to the elegantly charming inn. Its walls were of aged, rough-hewn logs, its furnishings rich and mellow. It was the perfect getaway.

Each drawn by his own interests, the jurors quickly dispersed. Some went inside to the game room, others went directly to the lake. Still others spread out along the veranda, settling into oversized cushioned deck chairs. Abby was about to join the latter group when Ben approached. A spanking clean volleyball rested between his wrist and his hip.

"Up for a game?" he asked. There was just enough of a challenge in his voice to counter hesitation, had he found it. But she had none. It had been a long few days of sitting for what seemed to be hours on end. Even the morning runs had barely tapped her well of pent-up energy. She was used to far more physically active days.

"Sure," she exclaimed. "Any other takers?"

"Tom and Richard will be out in a minute. They're seeing who else wants to play. I passed Patsy inside. She seemed to be looking for someone but said she may be out later. Do you think any of the other women would be interested?"

"I'll check. Where's the game?"

"Out back. In . . . . say . . . ten minutes?"

"Meet you there." She smiled at him, feeling better than she had all day.

The game was just what she needed. She'd only been able to con one other female into playing—tall, thin Anne Marie, whose initial shyness had eased over the past few days to reveal a woman with a streak of wry humor. And did she ever know how to serve a volleyball. . . .

"Where did you learn to play that way, Anne?" Abby asked, after three straight points had shocked the all-men's team on the far side of the net.

"I was drafted."

"The *army?*"

Anne Marie shook her head. "Central High. It was a choice between basketball . . . and this. This seemed the lesser of the evils." And she fisted the ball a fourth time. This time, though, the opposition was prepared. By the time the game finally ended many more points down the road, both sides had earned the frosty lemonade that a beaming Patsy helped serve.

"Not bad at all," Ben grinned, easing down onto the grass not far from Abby. While the game had been in progress, she'd been too busy to concentrate on him. Now she noted the way his hair fell in damp swaths onto his forehead and the way he'd rolled his sleeves to reveal a breathtaking strength of forearm. With his shirttails hanging out over his jeans and the heat of exertion giving added color to his already healthy complexion, he had a boyish look that pulled at her heartstrings.

"It was fun," she murmured breathlessly.

"It was. . . . You're a good sport."

"You mean that you're glad I didn't cry when we lost?" she teased.

"I mean that you put up a good, clean fight. Next time you can be on *my* team." He beamed.

Abby's insides flip-flopped madly. She'd be on Ben's team any day, she mused, then shut her eyes to his bewitchment and lay back on the grass with an emphatic sigh. "It's nice here, isn't it?" The sun was a warm foil for the crisp fall air. "I could almost forget the circumstances."

"Tell me, Abby," Ben asked, his voice suddenly closer. "What would you be doing on a normal Saturday?" When she opened her eyes, she found him lying on his stomach, propped on his elbows, his face inches away.

Swallowing hard, she closed her eyes again and tried to concentrate on what she *would* normally have been doing. It seemed a world away. "I teach a class in the mornings, then the afternoons . . . well . . . you know . . . the usual lazy Saturday types of things."

"What kind of class?"

"It's a course on natural childbirth. When I first came here, I met loads of mothers who were expecting second and third children and were interested in trying it naturally. At the time there were no formal classes. Now they drive for miles to attend every week."

"Natural childbirth . . ."

She could hear it in his voice, that pensiveness that meant he was adding another piece to the puzzle of her life. Opening her eyes, she sent him a warning he promptly ignored.

"You believe in natural childbirth?" he asked softly.

"I believe that it's right for some women and that those women should have the benefit of proper preparation. For some women though, natural childbirth is all wrong."

"Would *you* want it?"

Something about the way he looked at her made her pulsepoint throb. "I'm not really sure," she managed to say. "It would depend, I guess."

"On what?"

"On whether my . . . my husband wanted to be part of it. Half of its beauty is that a husband and wife work together."

Ben didn't say anything, seeming lost in her eyes as she was lost in his. She could see him as that type of man, wanting to share those precious moments with his wife, and she felt a sudden wave of envy for the woman who would one day have him.

"What . . . what about you, Ben?" she asked unsteadily. "What would you be doing today if you weren't here now?"

As if freeing himself from a trance, he blinked once and took a deep breath. "I have some Saturday morning classes too. Nothing as exciting as natural childbirth though."

"You're making fun of me," she chided.

"I'm serious." And he was. "There's something much more *real* about what you teach. I think it's wonderful."

This time Abby couldn't look away, but was held by the silver intensity of Ben's gaze. She felt as though she'd known him for years, as though they'd been friends first, then lovers. She felt as though he could see into her, know what she wanted in life even more than she did. She felt perfectly naked and utterly vulnerable.

"Don't look at me like that," she pleaded in a whisper.

"Why not?" He inched closer.

"It . . . it makes me . . . uncomfortable. . . ."

"What if I said that I couldn't help myself?"

"Then I wouldn't believe you, Benjamin Wyeth." She groped at reality, trying to talk herself out of helplessness. "You're a political scientist, a man of reason, not impulse."

He frowned endearingly. "Funny, I used to think

so, too. But lately . . . *very* lately . . . I've begun to wonder. You're a woman who inspires irrational thought."

"I do not—"

"You do—the way you look at me with those big hazel eyes of yours, the way you smile and talk. Abby—"

"Shhh! Please, Ben. Don't talk that way." On a burst of resolve, she tried to roll away but he put a hand on her far side and stopped her. "This is crazy," she gasped, finding her body trapped by his.

"Don't you think I've told myself that?" he asked hoarsely. "What else do you think kept me from going after you the other night? I keep saying it's crazy . . . but I still want you." He paused, his molten gaze searing her features one by one before casting its heat deeper. "You know that, don't you?"

How could she help but know it when her insides felt on fire and her blood raced in a wild torrent through her veins. She wanted Ben too; there was no doubt in her mind. Nor was there doubt that she was as crazy as he if she thought it would be right . . . under the circumstances.

"No . . ." she whispered, but her eyes dropped to his lips, and she mindlessly reached to touch them. They were firm and strong, warm and willing. Her fingertips traced their manly shape in the exploration of the blind. Then, burned by the flame that leaped between them, she sucked her breath in sharply and tore her hand away. "No!" she cried more forcefully. In truth, she was terrified by the strength of the attraction she felt.

Startled by her tone, Ben eased back. "Shhhh. It's all right, Abby," he said, gentling her softly, all the while studying her expression through a quizzical one of his own. Then he slowly pushed himself away and sat up. Knees bent, arms crossed atop them, he looked out over the lake and took several deep, calming breaths.

Abby, too, sat up, but she never took her eyes from the broad-shouldered man beside her. When he sighed in frustration, she wanted to ease it. When he hung his head in disquietude, she wanted to reach out. But she did nothing until he turned to look at her at last. Then she nearly jumped.

"I could use that swim. Care to join me?" His voice was husky, but otherwise he seemed well in control.

Abby was less so. "I . . . uh, no. I think I'll sit this one out." *Swim* with him? How could she *ever* handle that? She doubted the lake could be cool enough to douse the heat she knew she would feel. Rather she'd sit here and give herself time to recover from this most recent attack of desire.

To her chagrin, she realized too late that she may have picked the greater of two evils. For, several minutes after disappearing into the lodge, Ben re-emerged to swim . . . with a towel thrown over his shoulder . . . and a positively devastating pair of slim-fitting navy trunks molded low on his hips.

Fortunately, he was preoccupied. Head down, he descended the long embankment to the waterside. His stride was an even one, the mark of the athlete. As she watched with a gnawing hunger, Abby was struck by the firmness of him, his long, lean length, the muscles that flexed minimally with movement. He was masculinity in motion, and the sight of him made her gasp for air.

When he reached the waterside, he dropped his towel onto a log, waded into the water up to his thighs, then swung his arms up in a continuous arc and dove forward. Abby sat straight, her own arms clasped convulsively around her knees as she followed the progress of his powerful stroke. His arms rotated smoothly, his legs barely broke the surface with their kick. His head turned rhythmically for air, and she wondered how he could be breath that much more easily than she was at that mome .

He must be a kind of demon, she mused, to be able to affect her like this. It simply wasn't fair! Why couldn't she respond to Sean this way, with the simplest look eliciting a sensual response? This was a jury, a *jury*, she told herself again. How could she possibly yield to the temptation of one Benjamin J. Wyeth? Any way she looked at it, it seemed totally improper.

But she still wanted him. No amount of reasoning could convince her otherwise. She wanted to explore that sinewed body, to know the texture of his skin and the feel of his strength beneath her hands. She ached to stretch out beside him and mold her softer curves to the straightness of his manly lines. Oh, yes, she wanted him . . . and in the eddy of desire there was only one thought that kept her sane. It was neither the life that awaited her at the trial's end nor knowledge of the gravity of her current duty. Rather it was the prospect of a woman awaiting Ben . . . and the fear that for him Abby was nothing more than a few moments' release from the tension of their circumstances.

Wallowing in this strange obsession, she lost track of the time. She was aware of others wandering around the grounds of the lodge, occasionally crossing her line of vision—a line that led straight to the lake. She smiled once, nodded twice, but couldn't move from the spot despite her inner torment.

Finally Ben swam toward shore, tossed his head back and emerged from the shallows to reach for his towel. His body glistened in the late afternoon sun; she wished she were the one drying it. But he seemed oblivious to her still as he briskly toweled his chest and arms. Then, wrapping the towel around his neck and tugging on its ends distractedly, started back toward the lodge, seeming as preoc .pied as he'd been on the walk down.

Abby held her breath, fearful that he'd hear the thunder of her heartbeat. She'd never know what actually did stop him, only knew that when he drew even with where she sat he paused, looked up, and stared. Not even the closeness of his damp body could lure her eyes from his. She was sucked in, held captive and released only when he rubbed one end of the towel across his brow and moved on.

Shaken, she sat for a little longer. But no amount of soul searching could alter the fact that to surrender to what she felt would be irresponsible. She'd never been one to do things on impulse. And now was certainly not the time to start.

Motivated at last by determination, she jumped to her feet and strode to the veranda, where she retrieved the bag she'd brought, settled into a free chair, curled her legs under her, and opened her book.

Fortunately it was easy reading, a popular novel she'd begun the night before. She tuned out all movement around the lodge, intent only on immersing herself in the lives of the characters. And she was successful. For when Louise tapped her on the shoulder and informed her that the ribs were just about done, hence the barbecue about to begin in a clearing on the far side of the lodge, she was startled. Feeling definitely refreshed by the hour's respite and proud of herself as well, she joined the others for a feast of not only ribs, but chicken and steak, sweet corn, potatoes, and three different kinds of salad. In some ways she was relieved when Ben kept his distance. They both needed time to let reason prevail.

Much to her satisfaction, Abby enjoyed herself. Not that she didn't with Ben—but that was half heaven, half hell. Here, though, she relaxed with a group of her fellows, finding, one by one, things to like in each. Perhaps having finally accepted that they would indeed be together for a while, they'd begun to open up, talking about the jobs they held, even their families. Abby found herself laughing gaily more than once in response to a personal story told by one of the others.

Moreover, she couldn't help but be buoyed by Patsy, who seemed to have taken upon herself to work with the staff of the lodge, running to and from the kitchen putting refills of food on the long buffet table, grinning radiantly at everyone, her cheeks flushed with pleasure.

"What's this about designing skiwear? I think you've found your calling here," Abby whispered while Patsy dispensed the carrot coleslaw.

Patsy's eyes glowed. "You should only know."

"But aren't you going to eat anything yourself?"

"Oh . . . I'll catch something in a couple of minutes."

"Patsy . . ." Abby eyed her suspiciously.

"This is fun!" the other replied happily. "I'm really glad we came." Then she lowered her voice. "Now, if you'll move on Miss Barnes so these other poor folk can get some food . . ."

Finding Patsy's effervescence contagious, Abby had moved on and enjoyed the meal. When it was over, though, she set out by herself toward the waterside. It wasn't enough to be sated by food and pleasant company. There was still Ben.

"Come on, Abby. Let's take a ride."

She whirled around in time to see the man of the moment capture her hand. "A ride? What kind of ride?"

"A canoe ride. Why don't we take one out?" He'd asked her, yet she sensed he'd made a statement. Though he was outwardly his charming self, there was a thread of intensity just below the surface that suggested he wouldn't take no for an answer.

"Isn't . . . isn't it getting kind of late?"

"We've still got close to an hour."

"But it's getting dark."

His lips curved into a lopsided smile. "What's wrong, Abby? Never been canoeing before?"

"Of course, I've been canoeing. Not for years . . . but I'm sure I can still handle a paddle."

"Are . . . you afraid of me?" he asked, his voice lowered but bearing that same challenge she'd heard in it before.

"Not on your life," she exclaimed. Actually it was her own response to him that frightened her.

"Then let's go." Without further word, he led her to the place where several canoes were beached. "We'd better leave our shoes here," he said, waiting until they'd both done as much before resuming command. Easing the canoe into the water, he held it while she settled into its bow, then waded into the water far enough to free the craft from the sand and hop into its stern.

Then they were off, gliding through the mirror stillness of the water toward the far side of the lake. "Are you sure this is okay?" she called over her shoulder. "Won't they worry that we'll get away?" There was something delightfully free about slipping through the water as smoothly and soundlessly as they were doing.

Ben chuckled. "You can be sure we're under surveillance, but then, that's their job. I understand there's a motorboat . . . just in case."

Abby nodded, feeling decidedly lightheaded. It was a glorious early evening, with the reds and golds of sunset lingering to strew a vibrant path across the water. The air was still, the only sound the swish of the boat and its paddles as Abby and Ben stroked in tandem. To speak would have been to contaminate nature's silence; Abby wouldn't have dreamed of doing it. Besides, she felt safe this way. After all, what could possibly happen in a canoe? . . .

With Ben's stronger paddle setting their direction, they cut across the center of the lake before veering to the right and returning by a route that hugged the shore more closely. The shadows had grown deeper now, those spatters of red and golds having given way to the blues and purples of dusk. Seeking the last of the light, Ben headed them back toward the center of the lake.

Abby felt totally at peace. When, at a simultaneous moment, they stopped paddling to sit still and absorb the serenity, she thought there was nothing more natural. When she felt a jostling of the canoe, however, she twisted quickly around.

"What are you *doing?*" she cried out in alarm.

"Moving up." Crouched as low as possible, that was exactly what he was doing. Having safely stowed his paddle, he held carefully to the gunnels on either side.

"Ben! You can't move. We'll capsize!"

His attention was focused on balancing himself as he spanned another cross-plank. "Shhhhh. I'm concentrating."

"But Ben . . ."

Having reached the section directly behind where she knelt, he settled back onto his shins. "Turn around," he ordered softly, taking the paddle from her hands and stowing it by his.

"What—"

"Turn around," he repeated the command. "Just stay as low as possible."

"This is crazy—" But his hands were on her waist, moving her when she hesitated. Totally engrossed in turning without tipping the boat, she didn't speak again until she was on her knees and sitting back on her heels to face him. Then, hands gripping the gunnels and heart thudding loudly, she yielded to bewilderment. "What in the world are you doing?" she cried, looking up at his darkened features. He took her face in his hands before she could think to pull back.

"I'm going to kiss you right here, where no one can bother us and you can't run off."

"But Ben—" She motioned futilely toward shore.

"They're behind me." Sure enough, he'd positioned the boat so that the broad expanse of his back ensured their privacy. "And as you said, it's getting dark. . . ."

He held her face still, denying her escape. Then, waiting no longer, he lowered his head and captured her lips.

"Ben—" she forced a muffled protest. "Please . . . don't . . ."

But he refused to listen. His kiss was the gentlest, most intense of caresses—a slow and steady persuasion. It took every bit of her resolve to clamp her lips tightly together. This wasn't what she'd wanted when she'd agreed to canoe with him . . . and to think she'd thought herself safe from temptation!

When she tried to turn her head aside, his hands were firm and unyielding. Soft sounds of pleading came from the back of her throat, but he ignored them to stake his claim. When she took her hands from the gunnels to push him away, the canoe rocked dangerously, and she found herself clinging to his shirt instead.

And still he kissed her, caressing her lips with a

warmth she found to be pervasive. It melted her insides and curled her toes, leaving her breathless.

Then, with a soft moan of pleasure, he moved to place gentle kisses on her cheeks and eyes. "Kiss me, Abby. It's all right."

"But it's not," she gasped, eyes closed now, fighting a need to acquiesce. No longer could she smell the fragrance of autumn; rather the rich, male scent of Ben filled her nostrils.

When he moved his hand to trace the line of her jaw with his lips, a slow, sweet lethargy stole over her. Her fingers relaxed their hold on his shirt, her palms flattened against the muscular swell of his chest. The rapid hammer of his heart seemed to echo through her.

"This is insane," she whispered with a last breath of reason. Ben pressed another kiss to each eye.

"If it's insane," he growled, "why can't we stop? We're both creatures ruled by reason, aren't we?"

She had no answer for him. Much as she could voice one feeble protest after another, she couldn't keep her lips from aching for his again. It was a torment—his kissing her everywhere else—and she turned her head in an instinctive quest. When he finally gave her what she sought, it was his gain as well. For her lips were open and welcoming as she sighed a blissful surrender.

Abby had never in her life been as fully intoxicated as she was at that moment. It suddenly seemed impossible to recall why she'd been hesitant, when her body tingled so delightfully. And she returned Ben's kiss with an enflaming passion, subconsciously urging him to even greater heights.

"That's it, sweetheart," he murmured as his hands fell to her shoulders, then her waist, and he lifted her higher against him. With a low groan, he buried his face against the soft curve of her neck. "You always smell so good."

She'd been thinking the same about him. "I told you—"

"No, it's you, Abby. You're more of a woman than anyone I've ever held in my arms."

"Don't say things like that," she cried. It was bad enough that her body seemed beyond her control, that he made her feel precious beyond belief, but to hear his words and have to fight them as well . . . She didn't think she could do it.

She was almost relieved when he kissed her again and she opened herself all the more in reward. It seemed only natural that his tongue should slide past her teeth to seek its mate, just as it seemed only natural that its mate should respond.

Her fingers disappeared into the thickness of his hair, reveling in its vibrancy as she held him closer. With surrender had come an insatiable hunger; her whole body ached for more. Mindlessly she arched against him, resentful of the thin wood plank that separated them. If the canoe swayed, she was too swept up in passion to notice.

While his lips continued consuming her, his hands freely roamed the length of her spine. When Abby moaned in satisfaction, he grew bolder. His fingers spanned her sides and slid upward, grazing the sides of her breasts until she nearly cried aloud. Then, as though sensing her torment, he moved to cover her breasts, gently caressing their rounded form with a stroking that reverberated deep within her. She leaned closer, ever closer.

"It's good, isn't it, Abby?" he murmured against her cheek. She nodded, too breathless to speak. If Ben was bent on eradicating reason, he certainly had the tools, she mused through her languor. His lips knew how to incite fervor, his hands to kindle desire. And the sturdiness of his body was a haven when one's own trembled madly.

His thumbs tipped up her chin. "Speak to me," he ordered huskily. "I want to know what you feel."

Slowly opening her eyes, she met his. "I feel . . . I feel as if I'm somewhere else . . . as if I'm some*one* else. . . ."

His fingers worked lower on her neck, those thumbs now tracing lazy circles near the hollow of her throat. Her open-necked shirt presented no barrier. Nor did a remnant of reason. She only knew that she wanted him to touch her more.

"Is it that unreal?" he asked, resting his lips against her forehead for a minute before looking down at her again. His fingers had slipped beneath her collar to explore the skin of her shoulder.

She closed her eyes to the delicious feeling and let her head fall gently to the side. "Yes, it's unreal. I've never felt like this. . . ." His fingers moved lower and she felt herself swell toward them. When she moaned, he kissed her softly, barely disguising his work of releasing a first, then a second button. A little sound of excitement came from the back of her throat when he spread the shirt and touched her.

"Abby . . . Abby," he rasped deeply. His hands circled her breasts then cupped them fully. She felt the warmth of his fingers moving across her nipples, drawing on them until they stood hard through her bra's sheer fabric.

"Yes," she whispered, entranced. "Oh, yes, Ben. So good . . ." The intimacy brought a pleasure-pain that surged through her with lightning-sharp brilliance, illuminating longings she hadn't known existed. Her own hands moved along his hard man's body with growing impatience, wanting to feel him, to touch him too.

It wasn't to be, however. From a far, far distance

away came an intruding noise, a voice echoing strangely across the water. "Ben . . . Abby . . . ?"

Their bodies froze; their minds struggled to understand the intrusion. "Damn!" Ben muttered, his voice hoarse, his breathing labored. "The bullhorn . . ."

As confusion gave way to comprehension, Abby gasped loudly. "Oh, no . . ."

"Abby . . . Ben . . . ?" The summons came again.

He clutched her to him, burying her face against his chest. "We're coming!" he boomed back over his shoulder, then swore again more softly.

Abby took deep, shuddering breaths in an attempt to recover her composure. It was a nightmare if there ever was one—having to face reality again. But was reality *this*, this sequestered life with twelve other people and Ben? Or was *that* reality, that other life awaiting her after the trial? And where did the passion she'd just shared with Ben fit in?

"I'm sorry, Abby." She heard his voice, thick and muffled against her hair. "Talk about demoralizing . . . to be on top of the world one minute . . . and then hauled down by a . . . a . . . chaperone the next. . . . Well, for a man who likes to think he has a handle on things . . . I feel positively . . . impotent!"

If only her own emotions were as centralized, she mused as she took a final breath before pushing back from Ben's chest. Head down, she slowly rebuttoned her blouse.

"Abby?" He tipped her chin up with his forefinger. "Are you all right?"

"Yes," she whispered but quickly averted her eyes for fear he'd see the extent of her confusion. "I'm fine." She wasn't ready for an on-the-spot analysis of what had happened. There would be plenty of time for soul searching later.

"Listen, Abby—"

"Ben Wyeth . . . ?" The bullhorn blared again, breaking the still of evening.

"Yes!" he roared angrily, turning to face the shore. "We'll *be* there!" Then he carefully moved backward, retracing his steps to the stern, where he picked up his paddle and began to turn the canoe. Abby shifted around and followed his lead. Between them—and the excess energy that had no other outlet—they made it back in record time.

Nothing further was said; the mood had been lost. Ben was quiet, Abby similarly subdued when they rejoined the others and prepared to leave. Fatigue from the day's outing offered them a convenient excuse for saying little. And there were mercifully no comments as to the goings-on in the middle of the lake. Either Ben's back had indeed protected them, or the light had grown too dim, or they'd been just far enough from shore . . . or their fellow jurors were indeed very tactful.

Whichever the case, Abby was too preoccupied to care. Very little penetrated her consciousness . . . beyond the image of Patsy running from the shadows beside the lodge, where the figure of a man remained. Patsy . . . whose adored ski bum awaited her. Patsy . . . lively, fun-loving Patsy. Had she felt the pressures of captivity? Was this her way of coping? For that matter, was it Abby's? Is that what her attraction to Ben was all about?

The darkness was a godsend, hiding her bewilderment from her companions during the ride back to the inn. Once there, she went directly to her room to try and make sense out of what had happened. She needed the solitude; in Ben's presence she couldn't think straight.

But solitude eluded her. She'd barely crumpled into the cushioned armchair when a firm knock brought her to her feet. There was no doubt in her mind as to who it would be. Ben Wyeth wasn't one to accept . . . impotence . . . for long, she mused. Nor would he accept evasion gracefully. With a myriad of doubts and a deep, deep breath, she slowly walked to the door and opened it.

five

"MAY I COME IN?" HIS VOICE WAS DEEP AND controlled, if taut.

"I don't know . . . I . . ." Before she could produce a response, he'd walked into the room, leaving her to close both the door and her mouth. She turned to find him standing before the window, his back to her, his hands thrust in his pockets. At a loss for words, she waited.

Finally he turned and her heart flip-flopped. His gray eyes held a hint of apology. His grin was decidedly sheepish. "I just . . . uh . . . felt like company. Saturday night and all."

In that instant it seemed to make perfect sense. "I know," she said softly, then hesitated. "What . . . what would you do on a normal Saturday night?" If it was a repeat of the afternoon's discussion, it had a keener edge to it.

"Oh . . . take in a show . . . go out to dinner. Sometimes nothing special. Saturday nights are great times to get into a good book . . . then stay up until four in the morning reading, knowing you can sleep late. . . ."

She nodded, understanding and agreeing. Hadn't

she done the same herself on many a Saturday night? Sean hadn't cared for such quiet times, had gone off in a huff mumbling something about laziness. But he'd always been back, full of forgiveness by Sunday afternoon.

"Uh . . . speaking of books," she grasped at the diversion, "how are your ideas coming for one on *this* experience?" For lack of a better place, since Ben stood right by the armchair, she'd let herself down onto the edge of the bed. When he turned and eyed her intently, she wished she'd remained by the door.

"The experience of serving on a jury?" he asked.

As opposed to the experience of seducing one of its members, she returned in silent response to his arched brow. "Yes," she answered pointedly.

"The ideas are . . . coming. It's a fascinating phenomenon."

She tipped her head. "With your background and the type of book you've written in the past, I'd think you'd write more of an overview—you know, the jury system in America, a jury of one's peers, the process of deliberation—that type of thing. Am I warm?"

"Kind of." He smiled for the first time and leaned back against the sill. Abby felt herself relax accordingly. "Actually I'm keeping an open mind on the thing. You're right; a psychological study of the dynamics of a jury would be a change for me. And it might be very exciting."

"Are you getting much from . . . from the others?"

"They're opening up. It's slow." He grew more pensive. "The initial division into groups seems to have been based more on age and occupation than anything else. For example, Bernie, Richard, and Phil spend a lot of time together. A restaurant owner, an employee of the state tourism bureau, and a realtor—they've got a common interest. And they're all in their fifties."

Abby listened closely. "It's been the same way with the women. There are fewer of us—five to your nine—but Anne Marie and Louise are close, as are Patsy and I."

"What about Joan?"

"Joan?" she asked, her expression as enigmatic as her tone. "I'm not sure just where she fits in. She keeps to herself most of the time—a real loner. I know that she's never married. And even though she's close in age to Anne and Louise, they've each got husbands and grown families. Perhaps she feels left out." She shrugged. "She seems pleasant enough. And it's not that she hasn't accepted the situation. It's just . . . that I can't quite get through. . . ."

"I know the feeling," Ben returned. "Brian is much the same way."

"Brian's a great chess player," she burst out on impulse.

Shifting to cross his arms over his chest, he scowled. "Now that would make great material for a book. 'Brian Kent is a great chess player.' "

Abby recalled what Patsy had said that morning about Ben's having observed her participation in that game. *Was* he jealous? His eyes were certainly dark enough now, she mused. Yet here, in the intimacy of her room, she didn't dare force the issue. "I really don't know him—other than through running and chess. He's one of your big question marks?"

"Well put," was his terse reply.

"What . . . what's wrong with him?"

"Nothing wrong really. He's got this kind of macho streak in him. It's as though he's constantly got his guard up. I think he may be the hardest to crack. Seems to feel that it would destroy the image to open up and talk about what he's feeling."

"Is that what you're doing—trying to find out what each of us feels about being a juror?"

He shook his head, his features softening again. "There's more to it than that. I want the general feelings, yes, but also feelings about day-to-day things. For example, how did you feel when the defendant was led into the courtroom that first day?"

Abby thought for a minute. "I think I was . . . intimidated. It's a very different thing to see pictures of a man in the paper, even to see him sitting in court during the jury selection process, but to *be* part of the jury and see him led in by guards . . . and to know that I'll be asked to judge his guilt or innocence . . ." She paused to catch her breath. "Yes. Intimidated."

"You see now," he grinned, "that's interesting. You're not the only one who's told me that. The others may not have put it quite as eloquently . . ."

"Baloney! . . . But what about you, Ben? What were you feeling then?"

"You really want to know?"

"Of course."

He looked her straight in the eye. "I kept asking myself how a guy who should have so much going for him has managed to blow it."

"But . . . that's implying he's guilty!"

"Not necessarily. I simply look at him and see a whole lot that other people can never even hope to have. It's too bad. You know . . . the dreams of money and power."

Something caught at her throat. "Is that what you dream of, Ben?" she whispered.

He held back a minute, knowing that to share this part of himself was to allow Abby closer than most had ever been. When he spoke, his voice was infinitely softer. "I used to. I grew up with nothing. My parents worked their tails off for every cent we had. They died before I could share my own success with them." He shifted to stare out into the dark. "As for money, I have all I need. Power likewise. My demands aren't great on either score."

"And are you happy?"

His gaze grew more distant and again he hesitated. ". . . I thought I had it all once. Then it was snatched from me for no apparent reason." He clenched and unclenched his fist as though struggling to let go of that old dream and its pain. Then he drew in a long breath. "Happiness is relative, I suppose. I've been lucky enough to find it in other things. . . ." His voice trailed off and he rubbed his brow. "At any rate, I look at Bradley and can't help wondering. He must have had every advantage in the book."

It took Abby a minute to catch up; she'd stalled on the mention of his wife. That had to be it, she reasoned. He'd mentioned her once before with the same sound of anguish in his voice, the same distant look in his eye. He must have loved her very, very much.

"It's interesting . . . what you've said," she picked up gently. "You see Derek Bradley from the point of view of your own life's experience. I suppose we all do it."

"It's inevitable. Take our friend today in the eggplant purple shirt."

She grinned, as much in relief at the return of Ben's humor as at its garish cause. "You mean George?" George of the wake-up green jacket that first night. *"You* take him. *You're* the one writing the book."

The corner of his mouth twitched. "I wouldn't take him far in that get-up. But think of what *he* must think of Derek Bradley, who walks into court every day looking as if he'd just come from his private tailor."

Abby chuckled. "I see your point. For that matter, Louise has a daughter about the age of Greta Robinson. It must be hard for her to look at the defendant and see anything but a rapist."

"There," Ben declared. "You've made my point."

"Then . . . what about justice? How can he possibly have a chance?"

"He's got a high-powered legal team for starters. And you can bet he's gathered together a slew of favorable witnesses. Then, of course, he's got twelve people. Not one. Twelve. Each of whom has sworn to make a decision based solely on the evidence presented in court." If she'd earlier doubted his impartiality, the chiding gleam in his eye settled the matter. He went dutifully on. "It takes a unanimous decision to find for either side. If one person sees things his own way, it's up to the other eleven to convince him otherwise."

"Or vice versa."

"That's right."

"And . . . if it doesn't work either way?"

"Then we've got a hung jury and the whole three weeks will have been for naught."

Abby felt the disappointment as if it had actually occurred. "That would be awful. For that matter, two of us *will* be excluded from the final deliberations. *That* would be awful!"

He shrugged. "It happens. But I agree; it'd be a real letdown after having gone through the entire trial." Yet as Abby gazed across at him, she sensed that the trial's end would bring a letdown regardless.

"It's an odd thing," she began in an attempt to express her thoughts without saying too much, "to be thrown together with perfect strangers for an experience like this. I . . . I assume that permanent friendships are bound to emerge."

"I assume." He wasn't making it any easier. For that matter, his expression had grown shadowed. Straightening from the sill, he thrust his hands into his pockets once more and wandered idly around the room. Abby could do nothing but sit and watch, wishing all the while that this were anything but a *bedroom*. Her imagination was far too active.

He moved slowly, weighed down by a private burden. When he finally came to a standstill directly before her, his features were nearly taut as his voice had been when first he'd appeared at her door. She sensed that they'd come full circle.

"Abby," he sighed, "what do you think is happening . . . between us?"

Looking down, she studied the way her fingers lay against her denim jeans. She'd avoided the question for far too long. Perhaps Ben was her conscience. "I . . . I suppose that . . . well, what with the situation and all . . . it's only natural . . ." Even as she hated herself for her hesitancy, she couldn't seem to do anything about it. How did one say "You turn me on!" in a refined sort of way? More importantly, how did one say it without inviting consequences that one wasn't sure one wanted?

"What's only natural?" he asked evenly.

"That we should . . . that there should be this . . . attraction."

"Attraction?" He chuckled. "Isn't that putting it a little mildly?"

Abby shrugged. "I suppose so."

Cupping her chin, he urged her gaze upward. "I know so, Abby. It's much more than a simple attraction that can be satisfied by a few stolen kisses. I need—"

"Ben—" she tried to interrupt, but he put a finger against her lips.

"I need you, Abby," he growled, seeming to begrudge the fact even with its blunt acknowledgment. "It may be in part the situation . . . sitting so near you, sleeping, *trying* to sleep, so near you." He raked a hand through his hair. "I don't know. But I haven't been able to think of anything except making love to you."

"You shouldn't—" she began, thinking of all those reasons against but unable to voice them. For the look of tenderness that suddenly softened his features did strange things to her insides.

"I have to. I lie in there at night," he tossed his head toward the wall abutting his room, "and think of you."

"It's pure circumstance," she argued weakly. "Once the trial's over and we've gone our separate ways—"

"But what about now, Abby? We've got another two and a half weeks ahead of us. What about now?"

Her pulse raced wildly. "What about it?" she asked, softly, unsure. Her eyes never left Ben's as he lowered himself to sit beside her. One hand slid beneath the hair at her nape, the other tucked a loose mahogany strand behind her ear and stayed to trace its delicate curve.

"I want you," he rasped. "We're both too grown up to be satisfied with anything less than fulfillment. I want to make love to you. Here. Tonight. *All* night."

Abby was stunned, in part by the suddenness of his proposition, in part by her inability to reject it curtly. When he drew her closer and kissed her, she was equally helpless.

If only he'd been rough in his hunger, she'd muse later. Then she might have put up a fight. But his lips were gentle in their aggression, instantly evoking memories of the afternoon's passion. Now the flames burst back to life, blinding her to everything but their glorious heat.

Then the phone rang.

"I don't believe it," Ben snarled. "Let it ring.' "

"They'll only come for me," she gasped. "Don't forget, I'm not supposed to be 'out for the evening.' "

It rang a second time. Abby was singed by the heated gray of Ben's gaze, daring to reach for the phone only when she felt the hands at her shoulders slacken their hold. Then she scrambled to the far side of the bed where the intrusive instrument rang again. Intrusive . . . protective . . . which was it?

"Hello?" she asked, then glanced quickly over at Ben. "That's all right . . . Yes, he's here. . . . Downstairs? . . . He's on his way." Replacing the receiver, she exhaled a breath. "It's for you. A call downstairs. They've been trying your room and took a chance. . . ." Clearing her throat, she looked up. "It's an Alexandra Stokes. She says it's important."

It seemed an eon ago that Nicholas Abbott had delivered a similar message to Abby. Then it had been Sean parading as her fiancé. He too had said it was important. Now . . . a call for Ben. Was this the same person with whom he spoke each night? Somehow it really didn't matter. Innocently or not, Alexandra Stokes had given Abby her best argument against Ben's proposal.

Ben apparently disagreed. Standing with an oath of frustration, he eyed her sharply. "I'll be back." And he turned.

"No, Ben. It's better this way," she protested, but he wouldn't listen.

Three irate strides took him to the door. "At least she didn't call herself my fiancé!" he barked in sarcasm, then was gone.

Abby's insides quaked when the door slammed. Then she stared at it as though hoping to find a solution written on its blank expanse. There was nothing.

Turning inward, she tried to imagine what would have happened had the phone not rung at that particular moment. It didn't take much trying. She cast a knowing eye over her shoulder at the bed, the roomy king-size bed with faint indentations in its quilt where she and Ben had sat moments before. The indentations would have certainly spread by now, had the phone not rung. But then, the quilt would have quickly been drawn back and the sheets would have borne the brunt of their passion.

Angry at herself for the crudeness of her thoughts, she paced the room in search of distraction. One distraction. Any distraction. Even the slightest diversion would do. A newspaper . . . she didn't have one. A book . . . she wasn't in the mood. Her radio . . . not allowed. Her journal . . . no escape at all; she'd only write about *him*. Inevitably her gaze returned to the bed.

Was it crude? When Ben had kissed her, there'd been nothing crude about it. When he'd held her and touched her this afternoon, she'd sensed something wild and beautiful. Was it crudeness that made her insides ache, that made her breasts throb now in testimony to his gentleness then?

Was it crude . . . this image of the two of them lying in one another's arms? Or was it beautiful? Everything in her cried out for that beauty . . . everything but the quiet voice of reason that pointed to the different lives to which they'd return at the trial's end.

"Abby!" The sound was accompanied by the sharp rapping of his knuckles. Then she heard the doorknob turn . . . and turn again in vain. "Abby! Open up!"

Lest he alert the entire inn to his intent, she ran to the door. "Enough, Ben," she pleaded, both hands flat against the sturdy wood. "Let it be."

"We have a decision to make."

"It's already made."

"Then you can tell me to my face."

He must have known how the very sight of him affected her. "No. Please. I'm . . . tired. I'm going to bed."

His voice came through more softly as he leaned closer to the edge of the door. "That was what I had in mind." Pure seduction.

"Good night, Ben."

"Abby?"

She sighed and leaned closer herself. "What?" she murmured.

"Let's talk." He paused. "Just talk."

"*Just* talk? Where have I heard *that* line before? It's second only to 'let me show you my etchings.' "

"I'm serious."

"So am I."

"Coward," he taunted her.

"That's right." She admitted it readily.

For a minute neither spoke. Abby sensed that Ben hadn't given up but was simply rethinking his game plan. She could argue as long as he wanted, she told herself. But she wasn't going to open the door.

"Abby?"

"Yes, Ben?"

"I'll make a scene."

Her eyes widened. "What do you mean . . . a scene?"

"I could *really* bang on the door. That would cause a stir."

"You wouldn't. . . ." She'd tried hard to get off on the right foot with her fellow jurors, and she'd succeeded. She couldn't believe that Ben would go out of his way to embarrass her—and himself—in front of them. The episode in the canoe was suspicious enough, she reflected with dismay. A . . . lover's spat . . .

would be downright condemning in the eyes of her more conservative peers. Did she really want to call his bluff?

"I'll do it," he answered her silent query in a tone of such confidence that she had to believe him.

"That's blackmail."

"I prefer to call it . . . friendly persuasion."

"You're being difficult, Ben."

"I want to talk with you. And when I want something badly enough, I'm willing to go to extremes."

"I've never seen you 'go to extremes,' " she chided, then caught herself short when she realized she'd only known the man for four days. Nothing in what she'd seen had suggested a violent streak. As for stubbornness . . .

"Shall I give you a sample?" he drawled softly.

She reached for the knob and slowly opened the door. Ben had one arm indolently slung against the doorjamb on level with his chin. "You can wipe that smug grin right off your face, Ben Wyeth. Don't forget, *I* can make a scene, too. And so help me, if you do anything *other* than talk, I will. How would you feel if it came out that the dignified professor attacked one of his fellow jurors?"

If she'd expected to sober him, she failed miserably. His grin was as broad as before. "Spunky lady, aren't you," he quipped as he strode back into the room. It was when he turned to face her that the grin vanished. "Close the door, Abby. I'd rather not make a public announcement."

Fearful of exactly what such a 'public announcement' might contain, she closed the door. "All right, Ben. Talk."

When she leaned back against the wood, he returned to stand before her. "Well . . . will you?" he probed.

"Will I what?"

"Will you let me stay?"

"Just like that?" she cried in disbelief.

"Just like this—" He reached to touch her but when she held up both hands to ward him off, he paused. Then he sighed in resignation. "Okay. We do it your way." Rubbing a hand over the back of his neck, he paced toward the bed, then turned. Abby had expected that he'd launch a rehash of their earlier discussion. She wasn't prepared for the curve he threw.

"What do *you* want, Abby? Honestly. I know you feel something, that you respond to me. But what is it you want?"

What *was* it she wanted? It was no easy question to answer. One part of her wanted to kiss the prince and have him turn into a frog; that would certainly solve her problem. The other part . . . honestly . . . it was hard to say.

"I want . . . I need . . . more time."

"Time?" Ben burst out. "We haven't got time."

"We've got three weeks."

"Less than two and a half now. Abby, you don't know what you're saying. If you feel something *now*, to wait for tomorrow can be tragic. Things happen that are often beyond our control."

There had been just a hint of pain this time, but she'd seen enough to understand his rush. It was the past . . . his wife's death . . . his feeling that their happiness had been arbitrarily snatched from them. But those circumstances were different. That had been his wife. Abby was . . . nothing.

She shook her head sadly. "It's not always that way, Ben. You were hurt once and maybe it's understandable that you should feel this way. But there's a danger the other way, too. Don't you see that?"

"I don't," he growled. "Why don't you explain it to me."

He was too close and she was all too aware of him—his height, his breadth, the rugged masculinity of him. It would always be this way . . . and *that* was dangerous. It would be far too simple to forsake reason and succumb to the force of sheer physical attraction. And the consequences of such surrender . . . well, she wasn't quite sure she could handle them.

Pushing away from the door and stepping around him, she moved to the far side of the room. Every bit of distance helped. "We both know that these circumstances are abnormal. It's bad enough adjusting to captivity and the daily doings of the trial. But to jump into something . . . into an affair . . ." She faltered, seeking the right words. "We each have other lives, other people." She'd been thinking of Alexandra Stokes. Not so Ben.

"Come off it, Abby," he snapped. "You're not in love with the guy. And you told me yourself that he didn't turn you on!"

Abby stared at him in astonishment. "Sean? I'm not talking about Sean. I'm talking about *your* life! The one I know practically nothing about. The one with an Alexandra Stokes who seems to call you faithfully every night. Don't tell me she's your sister!"

As seemed to fit a pattern, her outburst quieted Ben. His expression grew less reproachful, more insightful, almost amused. "She's not," he admitted gently. "So *that's* what's hanging you up? Alexandra?"

"That was an awful thing that just happened," she argued in self-defense. "To be in a man's arms with him trying to convince you to let him spend the night . . . and then be interrupted by a call from another woman. . . . You bet it's hanging me up. Who *is* she?"

He eyed her askance. "You're upset that I *took* it, aren't you?"

"Of course not!" Yet she did wonder. "It was for the best," she told herself aloud. "When I'm with you I sometimes forget that that other world exists. Her phone call was a timely reminder." She caught her breath. "Who is she, Ben?"

Ben had listened to her argument with an undeniably satisfied look on his face. *He* knew that she'd been just a little bit jealous. He also knew not to dwell on the issue.

"She happens to be my Sean," he indulged her quietly.

"Your Sean? What do you mean?"

Sighing, he dipped his head, then looked at her over the rims of nonexistent glasses. "Alexandra Stokes is a teaching assistant in the department. She's working while she finishes her dissertation."

"You mean, she's strictly a colleague?" Abby cut in skeptically.

"Let me finish." His patience was strengthened by clear determination. "No, she's not strictly a colleague. We've been seeing each other for nearly a year."

"You date."

"Yes, we date."

"Does she . . . does she . . . live with you?"

"No," he answered with a knowing smile. "She has her own place."

"Do you live with *her?*"

"Abby," Ben sighed, "if you're asking whether we sleep together, the answer is no. We've had our intimate times . . . but not lately."

"Why not?" she heard herself ask and was promptly appalled. Was this really sweet Abby probing a man's most private life?

His thoughts followed a similar train. "You're direct," he allowed with a crooked grin.

"So were you a few minutes ago," she returned, stating her defense for them both to hear. "You're asking me to share my . . . my . . . self with you. It's only fair that I know what's happening with your . . . self."

When he laughed aloud, she blushed. "That's what I love about you, Abby. You're so warm and open and so much more sophisticated than most. But there's still this shy side that intrigues me. There are words other than 'self' that would express your thoughts more succinctly, you know."

"I know," she scowled. "But that brings it down to the most base physical level. And that's what I'm trying to avoid! You understand what I'm saying; that's all that counts. So now, what about Alexandra? Why does she call you every night?"

"Why does Sean call you?"

"Sean," she sighed in exasperation, "calls because he assumes that I'm miserably lonesome. What about Alexandra?"

"Same reason, I suppose."

"You suppose? But . . . what does she expect to get out of the relationship? I mean, Sean expects that I'll turn around one day and fall madly in love with him. He just won't give up. Don't tell me that your Alexandra is doing the same?" Ben shrugged in a way that affirmed the situation. "You're kidding! She's *chasing* you?"

"Let's just say that she's looking for something far beyond anything I've ever promised her."

"And just what *have* you promised her?" Abby asked, feeling a strange sympathy for the woman who'd fallen for this tawny-haired Adonis.

But the indignation of her question only evoked a

110

smugness in Ben. "I'll tell you . . . if you come sit with me."

Her curiosity was piqued just enough for her to consider bowing to his suggestion. Then a furtive glance around the room convinced her that she couldn't do that. The only place fit for two people was the bed and she wouldn't make *that* mistake again.

"Shall we go downstairs?" she asked innocently, liking the idea instantly. In fact, she should have proposed it earlier. But then, she hadn't exactly *invited* Ben to her room.

"That wasn't quite what I had in mind," he answered, eyeing the bed suggestively. One glance back at Abby's face though and he knew he didn't have a chance. "Downstairs?" he repeated as if the word were punishment in itself. When she nodded her insistence, he sighed. "Downstairs."

That was what *she* loved about *him*, she mused then. The way he could be strong one minute and humble the next . . . the way he could first rouse her spirit then tame it in the next breath. He was such a large, overpowering man, imposing in so many ways. To see him soften and give her a point here and there . . . it never failed to touch her.

Side by side, they descended the stairs. Though Abby felt relieved to be freed from such close quarters, the absence of others even here was a startling fact. She'd half hoped for a swarm of chaperones. "Where is everyone?" she asked, seeing only the desk clerk in the lobby and a guard in the living room.

"It's after ten. That's past many a juror's bedtime," Ben jibed lightly. "Come. Let's go out here." Taking her hand before she could protest, he nodded politely to the guard and headed toward the front porch.

"Who was *he?*" Abby whispered as Ben opened the door for her.

"A new one, I guess. Poor guy's got night duty . . . and on the weekend, no less. Of course, so do we, for that matter. . . . Say, will you be warm enough? I could run back up for a sweater."

She shook her head. "I'm fine. It's sheltered here."

Ben led her to the far end of the veranda where a large wooden swing stood invitingly. It was lit by only the palest of light that filtered out from the inn. "This is nice," he mused, taking a deep, chest-expanding breath, "the fresh air."

"Different from the city, hmmmm?" She recalled those more hectic urban days of her life. "Where were you, Ben?"

He let himself down into the corner opposite that in which she'd settled. Each was angled toward the other, Abby with her legs tucked beneath her, Ben with his crossed at the knee, one foot controlling a gentle rocking of the swing.

"Washington. I did my graduate work at Georgetown and then taught for several years at American."

"Whew! You certainly picked the city for political science."

He shrugged his indifference.

"You don't think so?" she asked, surprised.

"I think that there's as much to teach and study and think about up here. I'm not unhappy I made the move."

Too late she realized that Washington must have been the scene of his personal tragedy. But Ben read her stricken expression and quickly corrected her misconception.

"No. We met when we were students at the University of Wisconsin. While we were married, we lived in Madison."

"I'm sorry, Ben. I seem to keep reminding you of that."

"You do," he agreed, but rather than anger or annoyance there was puzzlement in his tone. He quickly shook it off. "But that's another matter. You had something you wanted to ask me."

Something she wanted to ask him? For a minute, she struggled to recall just what it was. Then she laughed at herself. "You've done this more than once, Ben Wyeth. You have this way of distracting me until I nearly forget whatever was on my mind."

"We were talking about Alexandra."

"Now I remember." She tucked her arms around her and eyed him in confusion. "You surprise me, Ben. Most men would avoid the issue. You've brought it right back."

"I want you to know about her. There's nothing to hide. You were asking about promises, I believe?" He got quickly to the point.

"That's right. I wondered what kind of . . . arrangement you had with her."

Comfortably resting his arm against the back of the swing, he chuckled. "Arrangement?" He cleared his throat. "Our arrangement is a strictly dead-ended one. I've told her that many times."

"But she won't accept it?" How familiar it sounded.

"Nope."

"And what *does* she want?"

"Marriage." The word hit the air with a dagger-sharp edge to it, made so by the thinning of his lips.

"And you *don't* want marriage?" she returned more softly.

"No."

"*Ever?*" the devil made her ask.

Even the dark couldn't shroud his sudden intensity. "I've already been married. Maybe I've . . . gotten it out of my system."

Again . . . the past. Abby wanted to reach out to him, to tell him it could all be different. But who was *she* to make promises? She'd never lived through his pain.

"You've told Alexandra as bluntly that you won't marry again?"

"Oh, yes. She knows I won't marry her. But like Sean, she insists on carrying that last shred of hope."

The night's silence was broken only by the muted hoot of a distant barn owl. When Abby finally chuckled, she could have sworn Ben did as well. "The similarities are really funny when you stop to think about them," she began lightly. "Between my Sean and your Alexandra, we've got ourselves a pair of lonely hearts. Maybe, if we're lucky, we can get the two of them together. How would she feel about a doctor?"

"Mmmm . . . I don't know," Ben quipped. "I suppose a doctor's all right. She *is* partial to professionals. But what does this Sean of yours look like?" His voice deepened in self-mockery. "After all, Alexandra won't settle for a man unless he's tall, dark, and handsome."

Abby had the perfect antidote to Ben's tongue-in-cheek arrogance. "Then it might be a perfect match!" she exclaimed. "Sean is the epitome of tall, dark, and handsome. He's gorgeous!"

Her ploy had worked; Ben was less than thrilled. "That's just fine. But does he like blondes? Slim, willowy ones?" Revenge took silky forms; he deliberately drew out each word.

"I hate her already. What's a slim, willowy blonde

doing getting a Ph.D. in political science? Is she really dedicated?"

"Yup."

"And," she scrunched up her face, *"really* pretty?"

"Yup."

"Oh."

Ben regarded her quiet attempt to be nonchalant about it all. Then without warning he reached out and hauled her to his side.

"What are you *doing?"* she gave a loud whisper. "You said we'd *talk!"*

"We will. I just want you to be comfortable." He'd deftly fitted her under his arm and pressed her head to his shoulder. His hand stayed there for safe keeping. "And I want to remind you that it's *you* I want, not Alexandra."

"Uh-oh. That again?" she murmured without denying how comfortable she truly was.

"Yes, Abby. That again. Now that we've established that neither of us has other ties, what's to keep us apart?"

"What's to—" She started to raise her head, but Ben's hand brought it right back. "Try the unreality of this whole situation. How about *that?"*

"Is this unreal?" he asked, stroking the sensitive cord along the side of her neck and gently turning her face up to his. Even in the dark, his eyes held her spellbound. "Or this?" His lips touched hers lightly, sending ripples of excitement through her entire body. "Hmmmm?" he murmured mischievously. His fingers feathered the outer swell of her breast in their bid for a more comfortable hold of her arm.

Abby mustered what little strength he'd left her to put her hand against his lips. They were warm and strong, unfairly inviting. "I feel it, Ben. You know that," she gasped. "But I still can't shake the idea that it's being thrown together like this . . . that's causing the attraction." An image of Patsy, running from a man in shadow, flitted through her mind. "Captivity . . . isolation . . . close quarters do things to people."

"Do you feel anything special for Tom?"

She pulled her head back. "Tom? Tom Herrick? No!"

"How about Richard? Any stirrings when he's around?"

"Of course not!"

"There! It's not just the setting. It's *me*. *Us*. Damn it, Abby," he moaned in frustration, "you're grasping at straws. You'd respond to my touch whether we were in New York or Washington or . . . or Madison, Wisconsin. It *exists*. It's *real*. What's the problem?"

His arms had tightened, gently imprisoning her. She felt the warmth of his breath against her brow and wanted nothing more than to melt into him. But she was frightened. "The problem is *me*. I didn't expect this. I'm not ready to accept it."

Ben stared down at her, his voice dangerously calm. "And I'm not ready to accept that. So where does it leave us?"

She tried to wedge a space between them but she only ended up with her palm spread flat across his chest. "Hung jury?" she offered meekly. She half-wished he'd laugh . . . but he didn't.

"Not quite," he declared. "It looks like we'll just have to run through the evidence one more time."

It took her a minute to understand. Even then it was the quickening of his heartbeat that gave him away, an uneven thud beneath her fingertips. When she started to shake her head slowly, he captured her chin and held her still.

"It would be beautiful, Abby," he crooned. She

shut her eyes beneath the sweet torture of lips that touched each in turn.

Beautiful. As opposed to crude? Once more she was locked into the dilemma. "But it'd be . . . only temporary," she argued, catching her breath when she felt his tongue by her ear. "It'd be . . . giving in to an impulse that . . . scares me."

"There's no need to be frightened. I'm here with you." His voice was deep and husky, a stimulant in itself. Then his mouth found hers again and caressed it with such gentle care that she gave herself up to his keeping, if only for the moment. It seemed unfair to deny herself this simple pleasure. After all, he was just kissing her. . . .

But there were kisses . . . and there were kisses. Ben's kisses went beyond even *those,* sweeping Abby into a realm of pure ecstasy where time lost its meaning.

If only they had been able to go back to the beginning, to start from scratch with each and every kiss. But it didn't work that way. Anything that had come before . . . that day, the days prior to it . . . now added to the flame. They devoured one another hungrily.

Abby felt her whole body come to life. A slow sizzle worked its way through her veins, making her forget all reality but this man and his magnificence. Unknowingly, she slid her arms around his neck and arched against him.

His hands easily accommodated her, tracing her curves from thigh to hip to breast in eager exploration. And she gave him ready access, craving more with each passing second.

"Ben . . ." she sighed her exhilaration against the manly shadow of his beard.

"Feel nice?"

"Mmmmm." She felt as if she were drunk.

"See how this is," he whispered, easing her back

just enough to unbutton her blouse and shower kisses on her neck and throat. When his lips touched the top swell of her breast, she sucked her breath in sharply.

Eyes closed, lost in sensation, she whispered his name again. She felt his hands on her breasts, stroking them softly, his thumbs circling each nipple, creating peaks without touching. But she wanted him to touch. "Please . . . !" she cried softly.

This was one of the things that had been missing with Sean, this mind-numbing whirl of sensual pleasure. For that matter, she'd never *before* known this yearning to be totally devoured by another. But she knew it now and she urged Ben closer.

His fingers slid lower gently to draw back the gossamer cup of her bra until her naked breast filled his hand. Even the darkness couldn't dull the creamy sheen of her firm, rounded flesh.

"You're so very, very beautiful," he rasped softly. She opened her eyes and met his admiring gaze. While he stared at her, he circled her breast again, sampling its smoothness until she felt her insides begin to burn with frustration.

"Please, Ben . . . touch me . . ." she begged in a nearly inaudible whisper.

"Like this?" he asked, fascinated by her rapt expression when he took her tautened nipple between his fingers and rolled it gently from side to side.

"That's right. Oh, yes," she gasped. "That's right. . . ."

"And this?" Lowering his head, his tongue replaced his fingers, tormenting that turgid bud with its moistness until she cried out again. The knot deep in her belly had grown painful. There was only one way to ease it.

Ben's hand slid down her body, returning by the inside of her thigh and lingering to stroke that spot from which fulfillment would have to come. Abby gave a helpless moan and moved against his hand. Then, too soon, it was gone.

"Oh . . . babe . . . what is it you want?" he groaned, his voice thick with arousal. The faint tremor of his hands as they framed her face attested to the force of his own flaring need and the price he paid to control it. "Do you know now, Abby? What do *you* want?" It was the same question he'd greeted her with earlier. Then she'd been in doubt. No longer so.

"Love me, Ben," she cried, opening her eyes with the plea. "Please love me!"

Raw emotion had seized control of her. The moment was one of wild desire. It was only when Ben's body grew taut beneath her hands that she even realized what she'd said.

By then, though, it was too late. The damage had been done.

six

"LOVE ME, BEN," SHE'D CRIED IN THE DIZZYING heat of passion, but it seemed her plea had turned him off. Now Abby struggled to understand why. "Love me," she'd begged. Was it that wrong?

She couldn't know that silence hid the pain that would have been in his voice, that darkness hid the extent of the sorrow in his eyes. Yet, heart pounding, she did know of his withdrawal. His body seemed that of a stranger.

When he allowed a small space to come between them, the last of the spark fizzled and died. She sat, overwhelmed and unable to move, while hands suddenly cool and clinical repaired the havoc they'd wreaked with her clothing. Then he stared at her grimly.

"Love me," she'd asked what seemed an age ago. Now his answer was blunt.

"I can't do that, Abby," he said quietly. "I'm sorry." The hardness of his tone belied the apology, as did the seeming absence of all feeling in him. His withdrawal was emotional as well as physical, and hence twice as hurtful.

Abby felt suddenly violated. Cringing further back

toward her corner, she hugged herself protectively. Her breath came in ragged gasps. "Wh-what?" she whispered, devastated.

"That's the one thing I can never do. Anything else—"

"But you've been arguing—"

"I'll *make* love to you," he interrupted curtly. "There's a difference. . . . A critical one." He first sat forward then rose to stand taut and straight. Only the deep breath he took showed any sign of feeling. If there was regret, it was deeply buried in fatigue. "Perhaps you're right. You *do* need time. If you decide you can accept what I have to offer, I'll be here."

In a state of shock, Abby watched him return alone the way they'd come together. The night swallowed him quickly. Only the harsh closing swing of the front door betrayed his destination.

Then there was silence, abrupt and total. Gone were the sounds of pleasure, the gasps and whispers and soft moans that had been so recently. Even the owl was silent. There was only the melancholy creak of the veranda swing as it recovered from Ben's abrupt departure.

Bewilderment held Abby immobile. Then, when the haze of raw emotion finally began to lift, she understood. "Love me, Ben," she'd cried.

Love! She'd meant it figuratively; he'd taken it literally. But there was no confusion as to his vow, not the slightest chance of a misunderstanding. The one thing he wouldn't do was to give her his love.

But then . . . she didn't want that! She and Ben were simply two people thrown together in a situation of mutual attraction. Nothing more. She had no more desire to fall in love than he had. After all, she had her job, her house, her friends. . . .

Why, then, she asked herself, as she idly swung back and forth, had she begged Ben to make love to her? Had she simply been driven by the force of an awesome physical attraction . . . or was there something more?

Refusing to consider the alternatives, she hastily rose and retraced her steps along the veranda and back into the inn, where the scene was much as she'd found it on the way out. This time, though, it was she who nodded in passing to the guard. There seemed no one else about.

Relieved that Ben must have gone upstairs, she took that route herself. But was she relieved? Or disappointed? Had one small part of her hoped he'd have softened and returned to find her?

Head down, she ran quietly up the stairs, slowing her steps only at the third-floor landing. Ben was there, in his room right next to hers. Was he listening for her? Was he aware of the hurt, the . . . abandonment she felt? Or was he so lost in his self-imposed lovelessness that he couldn't feel for others?

Somehow, try as she might, she couldn't believe that possible. Everything she'd learned about Ben Wyeth had pointed to a man whose warmth was genuine. And she refused to believe that his feelings toward her were purely physical!

As silently as possible, so as not to disturb that one particular neighbor, she let herself into her room. He was afraid! That had to be it! Afraid! The more she pondered it, the more sense it made. Here was a man who'd been tragically hurt once when the wife he'd loved had been abruptly taken from him. He'd talked of disillusionment and pain. How fitting that he'd try to protect himself for the future.

Fitting . . . and tragic in itself. For Ben Wyeth was a man to be loved wholeheartedly, and he was a man to give likewise in return. *That* Abby knew with her mind as well as her heart, though she was at a total loss as to what to do with the knowledge.

Frustrated and downhearted, she showered, then climbed into bed with her book. What had he said . . . that some Saturday nights he'd pick up a good book and read until all hours of the night? It seemed to Abby the only remedy for this night, when she knew that sleep would elude her. And Sunday mornings . . . they were good for sleeping late. . . .

This Sunday was no exception, despite the fact that Abby's late night had been only in part due to the book she'd read. Brooding had taken its toll and she slept until after ten to compensate.

Even then, she felt unusually lazy. And the heavily overcast skies were uninspiring. On a whim, she phoned the front desk to see if she might have muffins and tea sent up. When the response was an accommodating affirmative, she slid back down beneath the covers to indulge in several moments' idleness.

It seemed she'd no more than drawn up the quilt when she heard a soft knock at the door. Room service? So quickly? Jumping up, she threw on her robe. "Coming!"

"Abby . . . it's me," came Patsy's timid voice, and not room service at all.

Abby quickly opened the door. "Patsy! Come on in."

"I'm not disturbing you then?" the blonde asked, taking in the unmade bed and Abby's bathrobe at a glance. "I mean," she whispered with a grimace, "you're alone, aren't you?"

"Of course, I am! And you're certainly not disturbing me. I woke up a little while ago. The desk said they'd send up some breakfast. Shall I call and have them add something for you?" The thought of talking with ever-cheerful Patsy was a refreshing one.

Patsy tipped her head to the side. "Hmmm, that *does* sound nice. I've just come from breakfast, but I'd love a second cup . . . if you're sure you don't mind the company. . . ."

If her friend was unduly hesitant, Abby attributed it to her own newly arisen state. In fact, she usually did prefer solitude in the morning. This day, though, was an exception. "I'd love the company. What'll it be?"

With a cup of coffee added to the order, Abby propped herself against the headboard of the bed while Patsy settled at its foot. "I got worried," the younger woman began, "when you didn't show for breakfast."

"Oh . . . I was up late reading, and since there weren't any automatic wake-up calls this morning, I decided to sleep in."

"No running today?"

"Nope. It's a day of rest in every sense."

Patsy eyed her closely. "You do look tired. Is . . . is everything all right?" She paused. "I didn't get to see you when we got back last night."

The hint of speculation in her voice tipped Abby off; it seemed each woman had cause to wonder about the other. "I'm fine," Abby said more softly. "It was a . . . late night, that's all."

"He wasn't at breakfast either, you know. I thought perhaps . . . that he might be here with you."

There seemed no point in feigning ignorance. "No, Patsy. We spent a while talking last night, then went our own ways."

"On . . . friendly terms?"

Abby's chuckle held an undertone of sadness. "In a way."

"Only 'in a way'? Surely you can do better than that."

"Aw, Patsy, don't get your hopes up. Matchmaking isn't all it's cracked up to be."

"But you two are so perfect for each other."

Abby frowned. "Not . . . quite." She gave each word due emphasis.

Again Patsy grew hesitant. "Want to talk about it?"

Strangely Abby did. "There's not an awful lot to say." She shrugged. "You're right. He's gorgeous. He's also very bright and has a great sense of humor."

"And . . . ?"

"And nothing. We're attracted to one another but it can't go anywhere."

"Whyever not?"

This was the hardest to accept. Abby's gaze fell to the sheets, and she absently toyed with a linen fold. Finally she bit her lip and looked up. "Because Ben was married once, a long time ago. His wife died in some kind of fluke accident and he's never gotten over it."

Patsy's eyes widened. "You mean that he's still in love with her?"

"That's not quite it. And, mind you, I'm only guessing based on what he's told me. I'm certainly not a psychiatrist."

"Well . . . ?"

"He suffered terribly when his wife died. On the surface, he may have conquered the bitterness and pain, but he's determined never to open himself to it again. He wants nothing to do with love. Anyone who has a relationship with him has to understand and accept that."

"And what do *you* want?"

The question came upon her so quickly that Abby

had to struggle to shift gears from contemplation of Ben's mind to that of her own. "I'm not sure." She tried to be honest. "I do feel . . . something for him."

"Do you love him?" Patsy asked gently.

"Come on, Patsy. I've known him for less than a week!"

"What does *that* have to do with anything? With Bud and me it was love at first sight!"

"Speaking of which . . ." Abby was about to broach the topic of the man in the shadows at the hunting lodge when a sharp rap came at the door.

Patsy bobbed up instantly. "Here, I'll get it. You stay put."

Before Abby could even get her feet to the floor, Patsy had crossed it and opened the door, leaving Abby to wonder whether her speed had been in the hope that it was Ben at the door . . . or in relief that she'd been temporarily let off the hook. Whichever, it was room service, bringing far more than Abby had even ordered. There were eggs and hash browns, juice, toast, muffins and croissants, not to mention pots of tea and coffee, all of which Katherine Blayne insisted on leaving.

"Just eat whatever you want," she said with a smile. "And if there's anything else—"

"Anything else! You've got enough here for three!" Or . . . one woman and one very hungry man. For an instant Abby wondered if others had speculated on her relationship with Ben. Then she cast the thought aside as being unduly paranoid. "Thanks, though, Katherine," she finished with a smile to match that of the departing waitress.

When the door closed, Abby and Patsy eyed one another in amusement. "I hope you're planning to help me with this," Abby quipped, shifting her gaze to the tray that sat proudly on the bed.

"Uh-uh . . . I've already had something. . . ."

"Then have some more. Come on." She glanced at her friend from the corner of her eye. "If you help me eat, I promise I won't ask *you* any questions until . . . until we're done."

Actually, Patsy did have a croissant with her coffee while she and Abby chatted easily about the new ideas Patsy had for some sketches she'd planned to make that afternoon. When the last of the coffee and tea had disappeared, however, Abby returned as promised to the image that had nagged at her.

"Who was he, Patsy . . . that man at the lodge? Once we got there, you seemed pretty excited . . . helping in the kitchen and all. And then when we were getting ready to leave, I saw you with him. . . ."

"You saw me, huh?"

"Yes, ma'am."

Patsy grinned in embarrassment. "I was hoping to get away with it."

"Well, you didn't, my friend, though I don't know if any of the others saw. Who was he?"

"He was . . . working in the kitchen there."

"And you just . . ." Abby made a swirling gesture with her hand, "hit it off?"

Patsy shrugged, then nodded, her lips shut tight.

"But what about Bud?" Abby asked, choosing her words with the care of a tightrope walker balanced precariously between curiosity and accusation. "Wouldn't he be upset to know that you spent time with another man?"

There was a generous dose of love in Patsy's sheepish smile. "If he learned I'd been with someone else, he'd probably be furious! He's a very possessive man!"

"So you've said," Abby observed, recalling the very first time she'd spoken with Patsy. Then it had been an issue of Bud's not taking kindly to the fact of her sequestration; now it was an even more volatile issue. "What *were* you doing today with that man?" Her near whisper expressed her concern.

Patsy grew serious, then troubled. Looking thoroughly torn, she rose quietly and crossed to the dresser, where she nervously fingered the lace runner. Her voice came softly; she didn't turn.

"Some rules are made to be broken."

"I know that," Abby returned gently, "but aren't you playing with fire?"

"Yes."

"You love Bud, don't you?"

"Oh, yes."

"Doesn't it bother you . . . hiding things like this?"

When Patsy finally turned, her expression was enigmatic. "Yes, it bothers me . . . in ways I can't discuss. And *that* bothers me, too. But I can only tell you that love makes exceptions. . . ." She walked softly back to the bed. "Take you and Ben—"

"We're talking about *you.*"

"And I'm turning the discussion around to make a point." Patsy's smile held an odd poignancy. "I think you're falling in love with him, and if you are," she raised her voice and held up a hand when Abby opened her mouth to venture rebuttal, "you should consider accepting him on his terms."

Stunned by the simplicity of Patsy's solution, Abby closed her mouth and exhaled loudly. Futilely seeking her fortune at the bottom of her teacup, she swirled the last drops, sipped them, then replaced the cup on its tray. "You mean . . . I should sleep with him." Her gaze met Patsy's and the fair-skinned woman blushed in apology at the bluntness.

"Yes," she murmured. "If . . . you love him."

"But I *don't* love him, Patsy! At least I don't think I do." She threw up her hands in frustration. "It's so difficult to know anything under these crazy circumstances! The situation here is totally unreal."

"Is it?" Patsy countered, again more solemnly. "Is it all that unreal? Or is it simply different? After all, we can never know what the future will hold. Adaption is the name of the game, but love is the one thing that stays the same, regardless of how the game board changes."

"And you know you'll love Bud, and he you, despite other . . . men?"

"But it's not that way. . . . I mean, what you saw yesterday was . . . harmless. . . ." Suddenly uncomfortable, Patsy moved from the bed again. "And there's something else," she began more softly, "I think that we're all given tests now and then. For Bud and me, these three weeks are a kind of test of our love." She faced Abby abruptly. "Maybe so for you and Ben."

"It's different for us, Patsy. We've just met. And we're *not* in love!"

But Patsy wasn't about to accept defeat. "The buds are there," she teased. "I can see them in your eyes whenever mention of the man is made." She cocked her head and frowned pensively. "You know, there's always the chance that, even in spite of the wall he's built, Ben could change . . . particularly if you work on him from the inside. Break a few of your own rules here and there. Give in. Accept what he offers and get under his skin. Who knows," she added on a tempting note, "the prize may well be worth it!"

More than Abby might have expected, Patsy's words stayed with her during the next few days. There had been a thread of hope in them, and it was to this that she clung quite against her better judgment. If there *was* no love involved, the thoughts should have been irrelevant, she reasoned. Yet they remained.

She didn't see Ben again until dinnertime Sunday

night, and then he was pleasant, albeit detached. He wore a calm, studied expression, betraying none of the nervous flutterings his presence caused *her*. If she hadn't known better, she would have sworn he'd spent the day fortifying that psychological barrier he'd built; he seemed utterly immune to her.

He politely inquired about her day, then patiently gave a general sketch of his own. Both had been quiet—reading, writing, trying to relax. A small group of jurors had gone to a private movie showing; both Abby and Ben had opted out. Sean had called again, as had Alexandra. Nothing had changed.

Abby's dilemma weighed heavily on her mind. She seemed to vacillate: I love him, I love him not. On the one hand was good sense telling her she couldn't possibly be falling in love. On the other was her heart's gentle palpitation at the very thought of Ben.

She began to regard Monday morning's resumption of the trial as a welcome rescue from this personal quagmire. When the judges had been seated and the prosecutor stepped forward, however, she had second thoughts.

For Greta Robinson took the stand, commencing an emotionally draining three days of testimony— the young woman's own account of what had taken place.

Guided slowly, one question at a time, she systematically related the circumstances of her introduction to Derek Bradley three years before, the building of their relationship, their eventual decision to live together. She obediently described her own background, then the lifestyle they'd shared during the year they were together.

Her composure began to slip when she told of having thought she'd been in love but of having been increasingly disillusioned by a host of unkept promises, not the least of which was that of marriage. Re-

131

calling the escalation of tension between them, she was clearly shaken. Occasionally sipping from a cup of water, she described the disagreements and arguments which had led to her eventual decision to leave him. That had been three weeks before the alleged abduction.

Nor had those three weeks themselves been quiet ones. The witness testified that the defendant had called her regularly, badgering her, demanding that she return to him. But, having been hurt, she'd been vehement, refusing even to see him.

Very carefully in light of her obvious stress, the prosecutor led her through the course of that day when she'd been forced into Derek Bradley's car on her way home from work and taken to the cabin in the woods.

It was here that the worst of the ordeal began for Abby as well. Hands clenched tightly in her lap, she listened to what had to be a painful story for any woman to tell, much less have experienced. There were endless days of being bound to a bed while her captor stalked about before her, of being fed bare rations while he ate in style. There were times when she was alone, when he'd disappeared for a full day, leaving her tied and locked in, helpless, terrified. There were threats and there were beatings; she'd finally come to fear for her life.

And what had Derek Bradley wanted? He'd wanted her complete submission to his every wish.

Abby was totally engrossed throughout the testimony, so much so that at one point on Tuesday, when Ben reached out to put a warm hand over her own cold one, she jumped.

"Take it easy," he whispered soothingly, then shot a glance toward the lawyers momentarily gathered at the sidebar. "Just concentrate on the facts.

Remember . . . the prosecution is counting on your emotional reaction."

"But Ben, that poor woman is absolutely distraught! How can you not believe her?"

"I'm not saying I don't. But there's always the possibility that she's worked herself up for our benefit."

"That's a terribly cynical view."

"It's a realistic one. Think about it."

Hurt by his seeming lack of feeling, Abby looked away. But she did think about what he'd said, and she had to admit, albeit begrudgingly, that he was right. In fact, the more she thought of it, the more she was appalled at herself. Of course each side would try to convince the jury of its own case! And what *better* way than through an intense emotional portrayal?

It was late Wednesday when Greta Robinson finally left the witness stand. Even the facts alone seemed to have won her the support of the jury, whose drawn looks and very obvious disturbance expressed what words could not.

Counsel for the defense hadn't spared a thing in its cross-examination, posing one leading question after the next designed to paint the witness as a woman with a history of love affairs gone awry. In Abby's mind the tactic backfired, possibly because of the lack of conclusive evidence to suggest that the victim had either been consistently troublesome or unnecessarily provocative, more probably because of the way Greta Robinson maintained a humble dignity beneath the defender's relentless onslaught.

Even Ben seemed deeply affected by the time her testimony finally drew to a close. But much as Abby ached to talk with him, she didn't dare. For one thing, it was against the judge's decree. For another, she simply didn't have the courage to approach him. Shyness . . . uncertainty . . . fear . . . kept her at a safe and objective distance. The resultant sadness was her own very private burden.

Thursday saw a steady stream of witnesses being sworn in, offering testimony, being dismissed. There was a doctor describing Greta Robinson's physical state when she'd been brought in by police; there was a psychiatrist describing her mental state, as well as the continuing therapy she'd been forced to undergo. Then testimony turned to the tracking down of the defendant, starting with the Boston security guard who'd spotted Derek Bradley entering a downtown hotel, moving on to the police from Vermont who'd taken charge of extradition proceedings. Then began the flow of witnesses testifying against the defendant, citing instances of arrogance, insensitivity, even cruelty.

Fortunately for the defense, court recessed for the day in the middle of this damaging procession. Fortunately for the jurors, the sheriff's department had arranged for another movie showing that night. This time, fourteen people jumped at the opportunity for diversion.

Unfortunately for Abby, the movie was a love story of the four-tissue type—just what she didn't need. But it had been this . . . or brood alone. She'd really had no choice.

She'd taken a seat toward the rear of the small theater; most of the others had scattered nearer the front. It seemed a pattern, she mused in the several moments before the movie began. Deprived of the ability to discuss the case with each other, the jurors often withdrew into themselves. It was a pattern she'd come to understand and accept, even to share. There was only one person with whom *she* wanted to talk when the weight of the trial bore down on her . . . and that she couldn't do for more reasons than one.

He sat several rows behind, slouched in his seat, deep in thought with his hands fisted against his chin. Abby wondered about his feelings but could read nothing in his masked expression.

Patsy, on the other hand, was an open book, more resilient than the others and in this instance more enthusiastic. She'd accompanied Abby into the theater but had settled in a seat near the aisle, in apparent deference to her friend's pensiveness, when Abby had chosen to move further along.

The lights dimmed and the movie began. Abby found herself easily swept up in the story, a tale of love and betrayal, danger and tragedy in war-torn London. The first of her tears fell for the hero and heroine when they were torn from each other after falling passionately in love. She drew the second tissue from her purse when the horror of war, felt through the personal losses of these two characters, set in. Then, when happiness seemed finally within the grasp of the lovers, only to be cruelly wrenched from them once more, she pressed the third tissue to her lips in grief. At that moment Abby detected movement beside her. Within instants, a comforting arm circled her shoulders.

She recoiled on reflex, but Ben held her firmly, tucking her head back against his shoulder, smoothing tears from her cheeks.

"I'm so embarrassed," she whispered unevenly.

"Don't be," he returned softly but said nothing more.

Nor did she. For whatever reasons he'd chosen to come forward, she selfishly accepted his attention. No promise of fictitious happiness on the silver screen could rival the peace she felt just now.

His strong arm about her was protective; his

warmth seeped slowly through her. Little by little it grew harder to concentrate on the movie. Closing her eyes, Abby savored Ben's nearness. It was as if the dark of the theater allowed for such lapses; she felt no guilt at all.

When Ben's cheek moved against the crown of her head and his lips brushed her forehead, she opened her eyes to the inevitable fire. It was there; she didn't need light to see it. It was in the strength of the arm around her, in the ardor of the fingers that spanned the line of her jaw to turn her face upward.

"Abby . . ." he whispered, then kissed her with every bit of the desire she felt inside herself.

She met him halfway across the buffer zone they'd found. Here, in the darkness, there was thought neither of love nor promise, reason nor impulse. There were only the two of them, incredibly attracted to one another, grasping whatever they could before they'd be wrenched apart again.

"If only we could stay this way," Ben breathed against her ear.

Unable to answer him, Abby settled for pressing soft kisses to the chiseled line of his jaw. Then, skimming inward along the firm plane of his cheek, she met his mouth for another duel of desire that left them both breathless.

"Oh . . . babe. . . ." His fingers surged through the thickness of her hair and straddled her ear to hold her still. His lips explored every gentle curve of her face. When his work brought a smile of delight to her mouth, he traced its gaiety with his tongue before plunging into warmer, darker recesses. Then, chest laboring beneath the splay of her fingers, he reluctantly drew back.

"We'd better watch," he whispered, still holding her but now turning to face forward. Following his lead, Abby focused on the large screen. It held her attention for all of a minute before she grew distracted by the hand that gently caressed her shoulder. Reaching up, she drew it to her mouth and kissed its long, lean fingers one by one. When she released them, they fell against the firm swell of her breast.

Tempted beyond endurance, Ben gave up all pretense of concentration. He faced her again and kissed her quietly, deeply, drawing her as close as the theater seats would allow. Turning her in to him, he stroked the delicate line of her neck, then let his hand inch lower until it found her breast.

It was Abby's turn to moan then, for his fingers slid over her fullness, teasing her nipple until passion's current sizzled from that taut peak down through her body to her loins. But satisfaction was impossible. In a moment of frustration, she clamped her hand over his to still the torture.

"You're right," she whispered raggedly. "Maybe we'd *better* watch the movie." Her body throbbed in testimony to the crisis.

Ben was in a similar state. Straightening with an unsteady sigh, he left an arm as her headrest and took her hand to his lap. "What's happening?"

"Shhhhhh. . . ."

A new face crossed the screen. "Who was *that?*"

"I don't know. I missed just as much as you did!" And she could still barely concentrate because her thoughts were centered on the sinewed length of his thigh beneath her hand. Her fingers shifted slowly, in subtle exploration.

"What are you doing?" he growled by her ear.

"Shhhhhh!" Fortunately they were a distance from all of the jurors but Patsy, and *she* certainly wouldn't object to what was happening.

"Abby, I'm only made of flesh and blood . . ." Ben warned in an urgent whisper.

Flesh and blood . . . and seemingly miles of muscle. "I know."

"Not stone, Abby!"

"Shhhhhh!" Her fingers moved toward the inside of his thigh, sheathed in denim and noticeably strained. But at that point he clamped his own hand down to put a halt to her play.

No word was said. Drawing his arm from behind her, he took her hand and held it firmly on the upholstered arm between them. There were no more kisses, no more caresses. Neither did Abby hear a word of the movie's end.

Rather she thought of how good it had felt to be held again, even now how comforting that he held her hand. She thought of how much she had enjoyed teasing him . . . though she'd never played that particular game before. But she took pride in the knowledge that she could arouse Ben as much as he did her, that her touch could elicit the fiery response in his body that she very much wanted to elicit.

But where did they go from here? Awareness of the reality of the situation gradually returned, draining the pleasure from her bit by bit. In the background was a musical crescendo leading toward the movie's triumphant finale; by contrast, Abby floundered. By the time the credits had faded from the screen and the house lights had come up, Ben had released her hand and withdrawn. They'd emerged from the buffer zone.

Cowering from a coolness she didn't want to see, she averted her eyes from him. In so doing, her gaze fell on Patsy . . . Patsy and . . . and . . . an usher? *An usher?* They'd been seated beside one another, whispering. A distinct aura of intimacy surrounded them, and both seemed as oblivious to the end of the movie as Abby had been. Now, with the theater suddenly lit, the uniformed man leaned toward Patsy for a final moment before sliding from his seat and disappearing into the lobby. Patsy stared after him.

What was she doing? Abby asked herself in alarm. An employee of the hunting lodge . . . now an usher at the movie theater? Was it as innocent as Patsy made it out to be . . . as harmless? Or did the young woman have a definite problem?

Abby, however, had problems of her own. Determined not to look at Ben, she moved over toward Patsy's side. It was only when she reached the aisle that she realized Ben had gone in the opposite direction . . . and had vanished, even managing to return to the inn in a different van. He too must have wanted to end the moment there and then, she mused sadly. Or had he?

During that short ride back to the inn, she recalled his words. "If only we could stay this way," he'd whispered. At the time she'd been too wrapped up in his nearness to pay heed to his thoughts. Now, though, her mind was cool and clear.

"If only we could stay this way." There *had* been a sadness in his voice, and it went beyond a physical need. She was sure of that. He was torn! He was no longer able simply to erect a wall and hide behind it. Perhaps that had worked for him in the past. But now . . . now . . . he'd gone ahead and scaled that wall for the sole purpose of offering her comfort. He had to have known that he would find no physical satisfaction in a movie theater . . . regardless of how close they'd come. He'd wanted to be with her. It was as simple as that. . . .

As simple, as gratifying, as . . . unsettling. For what of her own feelings? It was one thing to second guess Ben's, quite another to analyze her own. *Was* she in love with him?

"You're very quiet," Patsy half-whispered as the van approached the inn. "Are you . . . angry with me?"

"With you?" It took a minute for Patsy's meaning to reach her. "Oh, that? No, no. It's not my place to be angry. I'm not sure I agree with you . . . exactly."

"I saw that Ben came to sit with you."

Side by side, they walked up the front steps. "Now when did you get a chance to see that?"

Patsy ignored the good-natured barb. "I saw. He's fighting it, Abby. You know that, don't you?"

"I think so. I just wish he'd . . . talk to me about it." That was one of the things that hurt the most.

They'd gone into the living room and taken seats in a corner to allow them privacy. Ben was nowhere in sight.

"Have you talked with him about *your* feelings?"

"Of course not! I'm not even sure what they are!"

"Well . . . he's obviously suffering from the same malady. How can you expect him to approach you with feelings that *he* doesn't understand, that he may not *want* to understand?"

"I suppose you have a point," Abby granted softly. "It's just such a touchy situation. . . . And the trial seems to be building up steam. . . ."

It continued to build. Friday's court session saw half a dozen additional character witnesses take the stand to testify to Derek Bradley's typical abrasiveness, his uncanny ability to charm when necessary, his dark flair for revenge. And the parade continued the next morning, with witness after witness conveying the fundamental meanness of the defendant's character. Derek Bradley, it seemed, if this collection of witnesses was to be believed, was a basically ruthless person.

Then, shortly before noon on Saturday, the state rested its case.

If only Abby was able to rest hers. But nothing was resolved. She was no closer to knowing the extent of her feelings than she'd been in the movie theater Thursday night.

It seemed, indeed, that Ben Wyeth was as strong-willed as the prosecutor claimed Derek Bradley to be. Ben hadn't approached her again in a personal way. Nor did he seem particularly affected by her nearness each day in court. For all outward purposes, she was to him simply another juror.

She began to wonder if she'd imagined the poignancy in his voice that night. Loneliness . . . that was what she'd *wanted* to hear. Had she read it into his tone?

What she needed, she realized, was a chance to *be* with him, talk with him, get to know him even better. Had they not been members of a sequestered jury, they might have gone off somewhere together for the day. Of course, she pointedly reminded herself, had they not been members of this sequestered jury, they would never have met! Yet for the first time she truly resented the limitations of their circumstances.

Time together was an indulgence, time alone a luxury. Nothing had come from running together each morning, little more from dining—en masse—at several of the finest restaurants in the area. Even the movie had proven a dubious interlude.

By the time she got wind of a mountain climbing expedition in the works for Sunday, Abby was willing to try anything.

seven

SUNDAY DAWNED DARK AND OVERCAST BUT did nothing to dampen the enthusiasm of the six who'd decided to go. There were Abby and Patsy, Brian, Richard, Phillip, and, of course, Ben. Ray was their official escort. A skilled mountaineer had been hired as their guide.

Dressed warmly in jeans and a jacket, Abby was one of the first downstairs. She was quickly joined there by Patsy, who appeared as excited as she. Abby knew the reasons for her own excitement; totally apart from the opportunity to be with Ben, a day in the wilds appealed to her. She hoped physical exertion would finally earn her a good night's sleep. As for Patsy, she simply beamed and said she was an outdoors girl at heart.

The group left soon after breakfast bearing backpacks filled with food conscientiously prepared by the Abbotts. Their destination was an hour's drive north of the inn, a mountain chosen both for its gentleness and its obscurity. It was relatively unknown, and therefore fit the sheriff's specifications to a tee.

Unpromising skies notwithstanding, the climate was ideal for Abby's purpose. With so few of the jurors along—and Patsy quite mischievously taking her place at the front of the line with the decidedly youthful and good-looking guide—she was bound to catch Ben at some point. When he quite deliberately fell into step beside her, she knew that her day was made.

"You're looking pleased," he commented, taking his eyes from the path long enough to toss her a look of amusement.

"I am. This is just what I need." In *every* sense.

"Ever been climbing before?"

"Nope. I ski . . . but there's a slightly different route to the top." As their companions gradually spaced themselves along the narrow path, she felt freer to talk. "How about you?"

"Ski or climb?"

"Either."

"Both."

Abby laughed. "I'm impressed. When do you find the time?"

"You mean," Ben lowered his voice, "when do I come down from my ivory tower long enough?"

"Now, now, *I* didn't say that. But I assume that you're very busy. What *is* your life like, Ben?"

Taking her hand, he led her over a particularly rocky area. His fingers were warm and strong, filling her with buoyancy. All too soon though, they'd returned to the earthen path and he released her.

"Oh, it's pretty regimented. I have classes every day, with student conferences and other appointments sandwiched in. Then there are faculty meetings and committee meetings and a handful of other meetings strewn around. Not to mention advanced seminars that are most often held in the evenings. Somewhere in between all that, I have to prepare lectures and do my own reading and writing." He took a deep breath and arched a roguish brow. "It's busy.

Not exactly an ivory tower existence." Then his grin melted Abby with its crooked flash of white. "But I do love it. And I have Sundays and holidays and vacations to do all the *other* things."

"Like skiing and hiking?"

"Like skiing and hiking."

"Were those things high on the list of priorities that brought you north in the first place?" she asked, eager to keep the floodgates open. The fresh outdoors, raw as it was the higher they climbed, seemed to have freed them both from past restraints.

Ben's gaze protected her from the chill. His eyes were as gray and soothing as ever. "They were really only passing considerations. I'd never been on a pair of skiis . . . nor had I climbed a mountain."

She recalled his mention of having grown up with few advantages and the jigsaw puzzle piece fit. Further, she respected the way he showed no embarrassment at confessing to what other men might consider a handicap. "Then . . . ?" she prompted him.

"I wanted a change from the city, wide open spaces, a quieter life."

"Quieter? From the sounds of it, you're constantly on the go!"

With her eyes glued to his face, Abby nearly stumbled on an exposed root. Ben's hand was instantly at her elbow. "Watch it, babe. It's getting rougher."

Not to mention the terrain, she reflected wryly. But nothing could get her off the track. "Wouldn't it be easier if you lived on campus?" she asked, realizing as she did that, had that been the case, he would have been a resident of New Hampshire and they might never have met.

He climbed further before answering. "As a matter of fact, I did rent a place on campus for several months when I first arrived. I found that I needed the distance, though. It's too easy to have an open door there, with people coming in and out all the time. I need my privacy . . . if for nothing more than to think.''

"Sounds very esoteric," she quipped, sending him a teasing glance. "What sorts of mysterious thoughts do you have?"

"Nothing overwhelming," he answered quietly. When a pensive look overspread his features, Abby worried that she'd lost him to those very thoughts. It seemed terribly important to keep him with her.

This time, she saw the root before tripping over it. The heels of her hands bore the brunt of her weight when she tumbled. Ben righted her easily.

"Are you okay?" Genuinely concerned, he turned her hands face up. "Nothing's cut. Do they hurt?" With the gentlest of motions, he brushed the dirt from her skin.

"They're fine. That was stupid of me."

"Not stupid. Your mind must have been on something else."

"Everything all right here?" Ray asked, finally reaching them from behind.

Ben assumed the burden of explanation. "Everything's fine. Abby tripped . . . but she'll live."

"Johannsen has a first aid kit in his pack." Johannsen was the guide. "Should I yell for him?"

Much as Abby was content standing with her hands held so tenderly by Ben, she couldn't warrant disturbing the others. "No, thanks, Ray. I'm really all right. See? Just a few scratches." She held her hands up for his fleeting inspection before tucking them safely into the pockets of her jacket. It seemed one way of preserving the memory of Ben's warm fingers.

"Are you cold?" Ben must have intercepted that

146

thought fragment, for he regarded her with renewed concern.

"I'm *fine.*" She smiled gallantly. "But the longer we stand here the colder it gets."

"You're right about that," Ray agreed, then brusquely motioned them forward. "Lead on."

Emboldened by her chaperone—perhaps in defiance—Abby tucked her elbow through Ben's and leaned closer to offer a stage whisper meant for Ray's ears as well. "We'd better do as he says. He's the one with the gun." She cast an eye back in time to catch the guard's dry smile. "Where do you think he's taking us?"

Ben's gaze narrowed on the path ahead. "Looks like it's to the mountaintop. He must have his men waiting there," he drawled, joining the game. He covered her hand with his own as they resumed the upward trek. Had it not been for the increasingly sharp incline of the trail and the guard following several paces behind, they might have been lovers strolling through the park.

"What do you think they'll do to us?" she asked.

"Shoot us at dusk, no doubt." He lowered his head. "We could try to make a run for it."

"Nah. I bet he's got the woods surrounded."

"Hmmph. You're probably right.. . . . We could split up and confuse him. . . ."

"Then one of *us* might get lost."

Ben eyed her with mock skepticism. "You? Get lost? I'll bet you could find your way out of a cornfield with your eyes closed."

"Then *you're* the one with the poor sense of direction?"

"Shhhh. No one's supposed to know that."

"You're serious.. . . ."

"Sadly so."

"Really, Ben?" She tipped her head away to look up at him in disbelief.

His expression was the ultimate in sincerity. "Really, Abby." Again there was no embarrassment. This was a man who recognized and accepted his limitations. She admired that.

He continued in a low, velvet tone. "I'm fine if I know the way by heart, but I have this knack for getting lost in new surroundings. Of course, if I had a pretty lady with a great sense of direction beside me all the time . . ."

Of course. That *would* be nice. A tempting, if improbable thought. Better to return to the game, she mused. Glancing over her shoulder, though, she saw that Ray had again fallen back. Had he done it for their benefit? The others were well ahead. This was the time with Ben she'd sought.

"What *are* your plans for the future?" she asked. Then, mortified at what must have seemed her implication, she quickly qualified the question. "I mean, will you stay at the college . . . or have you set your sights on other things?"

"Like . . . ?"

She shrugged against his arm, rather liking the feel of his solidity. "Like teaching elsewhere, or writing full time, or accepting a political appointment. Maybe you'd like to run for office yourself."

"Me?" He chuckled. "Not by a long shot."

"Why not?" She'd vote for him any day.

The path took a series of ragged twists and turns, forcing them to separate. At Ben's gesturing, Abby moved ahead, waiting patiently for her answer until they could walk abreast once more.

"For the same reason that I live off campus. Privacy. I like it. I don't think I could take the constant demand put on a politician by his constituency. I make too many demands on myself."

"And what are those?"

Eyes forward, he focused on the rugged trail. "That whatever I do, I do well. As a teacher, I constantly update my lectures. As an adviser, I take an active interest in my students. As a writer, I do as many drafts as are necessary to produce the best possible manuscript."

"And what about *you?*" she burst out on impulse, then went on simply because the damage was already done. "What about your private life?"

"What about it?" he asked, detached.

"What demands do you place on *it?*"

A light mist had begun to descend, dampening the foliage on either side of the trail as well as the earth underfoot. Feeling suddenly chilled, Abby zipped her jacket to the throat. Ben seized on the move to change the subject.

"You're getting cold?"

"It's really chilly. I wish I'd had boots to wear." Her sneakers were getting wet and did little to protect her from the fast falling temperature.

"Maybe we should turn back."

"For me? Don't be silly! I'm fine as long as we keep moving."

They did. For nearly another two hours, they trudged ahead, trying to rationalize the merits of exercise, of fresh air, of climbing-the-mountain-because-it-was-there. Though Ben opened up no further, he was quietly companionable and quick to offer gentle coaxing when Abby felt herself begin to drag.

Shortly after noon, they joined the rest of the group on the bald and drizzly mountaintop. Abby wasn't the only uncomfortable one. It seemed that Richard and Phillip had done their share of complaining, irritating Brian and leaving all three short-tempered.

Patsy had fared well beside her guide; but then, Patsy had evidently done this before. Not only had she worn long johns, she told Abby after the fact, but she'd come properly equipped with hiking boots and a water-repellent parka. Furthermore, a snug wool cap and a pair of mittens had mysteriously appeared to warm her head and hands.

Trusty Ray considered it all in the line of duty, ignoring the dampness, parrying the complaints, finding solace in the fact that there'd be no other fools on the mountain that day.

And as for their guide . . . Abby had to agree that, for all her fickleness, Patsy had good taste. Peter Johannsen, as he was introduced to her, was not only adorable and able, as his skill in ferreting out a sheltered lunching spot attested, but he'd taken to Patsy with a protectiveness that was almost reassuring. Abby counted on *him* to have the good sense that, if past example were a guide, her friend might lack.

Abby's greatest source of pride, though, was Ben. Even when things went from bad to worse, his composure never waivered. When the light drizzle evolved into a steady rain, he discovered a shallow cave into which they might retreat. When the temperature began to drop as quickly as the rain, he built a small fire from brush that he and Peter collected. When Phillip's grumbling resumed with a vengeance and Brian launched an unnecessarily harsh counterattack, Ben was there to negotiate a cease-fire.

Finally, with bones rested, hunger sated, and hands temporarily warmed, they stuffed the bare remains of lunch back into the packs for the long trek down the mountain.

It should have been easy with gravity their ally. Patsy and her guide led the way; Abby and Ben kept an eye on Brian, while Ray tagged behind earning his salary the hard way mollycoddling Richard and Phillip.

It should have been easy . . . but it wasn't. Muscles that were weary from the hike up were jarred with each downward stride. Clothing that had dried by the fire at lunch was now far wetter than before. Spirits were low, conversation at a minimum. All concentration was on getting home.

Then Brian fell. Brian . . . of all people. Brian . . . who ran each morning as though he were in training for the olympics. Brian . . . who prided himself on being the true athlete of the jury. Brian . . . who'd spent the better part of his morning and lunchtime reminding Phillip and Richard that they were soft, untrained, out of shape.

It happened so quickly that Abby was hard pressed to recreate the event later. She recalled Brian being several steps ahead of her, moving to the edge of the path to look at something, and suddenly vanishing. His hair-raising cry first told of imminent disaster. Within seconds Abby was on her knees near the spot where the sodden earth had apparently crumbled beneath his weight. Seconds later she was unceremoniously hauled back by an irate Ben.

"Get away from there, Abby! Do you want to go over, too?"

"He's down there, Ben—"

"I know!" he gritted. Then, finding what he judged to be a more stable spot, he stretched out on his stomach and inched forward until he could see below to where Brian had fallen. Impulsively, Abby followed his lead. "Abby . . ."

"There he is!" she cried, ignoring Ben's warning. "He's moving!"

Brian was indeed moving, appearing stunned but not seriously injured. He lay sprawled on the slick grassy slope some forty feet down from Abby and Ben. By some miracle, he'd managed to save himself from the rockier, lower portion of the ravine.

"Brian!" Ben yelled, cupping his hands to his mouth. Just then, Ray came on the run, took the situation in at a glance, and dropped down on the other side of Abby. "Brian!" Ben tried again.

At first there was no answer. The man on the slope simply shifted his limbs gingerly. When Ben called a third time though, he looked up.

"Yeo . . ."

"Are you all right?"

"Yeah."

"Anything broken?"

"Don't think so." He sounded more shaken than hurt.

"Can you move everything?"

Abby held her breath while Brian stretched again. He was sitting up now . . . a good sign.

"Yeah." There was an undeniable element of disgust in his voice. He was obviously embarrassed. Rolling onto his hands and knees, he struggled for a foothold. But his running shoes were as useless for grasping the slippery turf as Abby's had been for keeping her dry. With one step forward, he slid back two. A second attempt was even worse.

Hearts pounded all around as the five on top kept their eyes glued to the solitary figure below. When Brian tried crawling, each of the five cheered for him silently. But again there was nothing to hold on to. The wall of the ravine, its grass slicked down by the steadily falling rain, offered no more traction than a sheet of ice set at a seventy degree angle to the earth.

"Damn it," Ray cursed softly, then raised his voice. "Try again!"

It was hopeless, as Johannsen confirmed when,

having been alerted by the shouts, he retraced his own steps. Quickly instructing Brian to stay put, he turned grimly to Ray.

"If he tries it again, he's apt to fall further. And if he hits those rocks on the slide, he may get hurt. My rope isn't long enough to reach him, and there's no way he can scale the wall without some kind of help." He shook his head in concern. "I'll have to go ahead down the mountain and bring help back."

Ben joined the conference. "How about the side wall? Can he move laterally and get a footing?"

The guide sighed. "Not on that slate. It could be worse than the grass in this rain."

"And there's no other way out of the ravine?" Abby interjected, standing now beside Ben.

Again Peter shook his head. "See for yourself. There are walls on three sides and a treacherous downhill stretch ahead. And this ravine is only piggy-backed on another. No. We'd be better to pull him up."

Ray swore again, looked at his watch, and frowned. "We're less than halfway down the mountain. It'll take nearly four more hours to get down and back."

"We've got no choice," the guard stated quietly. "And the sooner I get going, the better."

It was Ray's responsibility, Ray's decision to make. With a grimace, he nodded. "You're right. Okay." He scratched his head, trying to work out the logistics of the rescue mission. Ben was one up on him.

"I'm staying here," he said. "You go ahead with the others."

"No!" All eyes turned to Abby. "I'm staying too."

But if her tone had been firm, Ben's was no less so. "Oh, no, you're not! You're cold and wet and there's no need for you to be exposed to this for another four hours."

"I'm staying."

"Abby, Ben may be right," Ray began, but she'd made up her mind.

"I'm staying. There are plenty of trees over there for shelter, and you can bring warm things with you when you come back."

"Besides, she's a nurse!" From out of nowhere, Patsy materialized to stand beside Peter. "It might be wise if she were here."

Abby's smile held instant gratitude. "Right!" she exclaimed, having totally overlooked that factor in her eagerness to keep Ben company.

"Are you sure?" Ray asked.

"She's going down with you!" Ben interceded, his eyes reflecting the ominous gray of the skies.

Ray looked around the group in a calculating fashion. "She may have a point though. It would probably be better to have two of you here. And since she's a nurse . . . ."

"Yeo . . . !" The distant voice came from deep in the ravine as a sharp reminder of their problem.

Ben dropped to his knees and inched forward again. "We're getting help, Brian. Are you all right?"

"Yeah. Just wondering whether I'd been left for dead."

Ben chuckled. "Not quite," he called. "The others are going down to get a rescue team. I'm staying here . . . with Abby. . . ."

Though the last was said on a reluctant note, Abby knew she'd won. Within minutes, she and Ben were alone on the trail.

Only then did he turn to her, his hands on his hips. "This is really dumb. You know that you'll only get more chilled."

"And you won't?" She pulled on the hat and mittens that Patsy had insisted on leaving with her. "Why is it that much worse for me than for you?"

"I'm a man. I'm more solid. I can fight it off better than you can. And, in spite of everything, there really *isn't* a need for two of us." He sighed. "You should have gone down with them, Abby."

"Too late," she sing-songed, then looked around for the best shelter. It appeared in the form of a broad fir just opposite where Brian had fallen. Its branches were dense, its trunk sturdy. Under its cover they'd be relatively shielded from the rain.

Ben called a word of encouragement down to Brian before joining Abby against the trunk of the tree. "Why does this seem familiar?" he murmured. He was still annoyed; she could hear it in his voice.

"It was an oak tree then," she mused, recalling that first Thursday night. They'd talked, then argued. Perhaps it would be the reverse now. "How's Brian doing?"

"He's fine. The only thing bruised is his ego. This won't exactly help his image. . . ."

His voice trailed off into a silence broken only by the steady beat of the rain. Abby shivered.

"You're cold?"

"No. I was just thinking of poor Brian. He's totally exposed out there. Do you think he's in any danger?"

"Not if he stays still. He's pretty sturdy." He paused, then cupped his mouth and yelled, "Are you there, Brian?"

"I'm here," came the voice of defeat from far down the embankment.

"Poor guy," Abby murmured again. "He must feel awful sitting there so helplessly."

Ben chuckled. "I know the feeling."

"You do?"

"Uh-huh."

"Well . . . what happened?"

Brushing a hand through his damp hair, he looked down at her. "I don't think I should tell you. It might ruin *my* image."

"Come on, Ben. I already know that you can't find your way out of a cornfield with your eyes closed. What could be worse?"

"Skiing?"

"Uh-oh. I assumed that you *had* learned how to ski."

"I know how *now*. But when I first moved here I had a time of it. After renting all of the right equipment and taking a week's worth of lessons, I thought I had a handle on it. That last afternoon I decided to try a new trail. . . ."

Abby's voice lowered to an expectant whisper. "What happened?"

"Oh, I did fine on the ski lift. But that was the extent of my success. Once I got off, I chose the wrong path and ended up on an expert slope."

She grimaced. "What did you do?" The sensible thing would have been to walk his way down. Somehow she sensed that that wasn't what he'd done.

"I . . . went down . . . in more ways than one."

"You fell?"

He nodded, his lips twitching at the corners. "Broke my leg in two places. Mind you, it wasn't funny at the time. I had to lie there in the middle of that damned slope waiting for the ski patrol . . . while these magnificent people zipped skillfully past."

Abby imagined herself in that situation and spoke the first thought that came to mind. "At least you weren't with a date." He winced. "You . . . were?" He nodded. "Oh, no. . . ." She laughed without quite meaning to, then apologized. "I'm sorry, Ben. It *must* have been awful."

Rather than being disturbed, he seemed fascinated by the way her eyes crinkled up when she laughed. "It was," he replied distractedly. "But . . . what about you? I've confessed to *my* faults. What are *yours?*"

This time it was her nose that crinkled up. "Oh, the usual. You know, I always forget to have the oil checked when I fill my car with gas, I never squeeze the toothpaste from the bottom like the tube says, and if you ever bring me a bunch of flowers, I'll give them right back to you."

"Now why would you do a thing like that?"

"Because I'm an absolute failure at flower arranging, that's why! Any man who wants to humiliate me can do it by bringing me flowers." Her eyes narrowed. "But I'm not the forgiving type. Better remember that!"

Ben grinned. "I'll try." Then he looked out at the rain and called to Brian again. "Holding on, pal?"

"Holding on. . . ."

Abby fumbled with the cuff of her jacket in an attempt to uncover her watch. When she saw its small gold face, she shuddered. "We've still got an awfully long way to go."

"Are you cold?"

"No, I'm not cold! You keep asking me that." When she met his gaze, she saw its humor. "Wait a minute. Do you *want* me to be cold?"

"Of course, not! . . . Well, not really. . . . Oh, hell!" He drew her closer. "Come here. *I'm* cold. You can warm me up."

He wasn't cold at all, she discovered in delight when he unzipped both of their jackets and pulled her against him. His body warmth was the fire they didn't have and it melded with hers to produce an extraordinary comfort against the elements. She was happy to say nothing, simply to rest against Ben with his arms holding her secure.

Slowly, the exertion of the day began to take its

toll. "I feel as though I've had two drinks already," she murmured against his chest. "I'm so tired."

"Just rest then," he crooned. Tucking her closer, he leaned back more comfortably against the trunk of the tree.

Abby must have dozed, for she came alive with a jerk when Ben called out to Brian again. Then he lowered his voice. "Sorry about that. I want him to know we're still here."

"No, *I'm* sorry. I shouldn't have fallen asleep."

"You're exhausted. Not been sleeping well?" His lips were warm against her forehead, reminding her of exactly *why* she hadn't slept well.

"Mmmm . . . so-so."

"Must be a common ailment. Maybe it's the beds."

"I doubt it." Certainly not . . . unless one counted the emptiness of them.

"Or the noise."

She quite deliberately rubbed her cheek against his chest when she shook her head. "Not quite." The inn was like a tomb after ten.

"Don't tell me you're as frustrated as I am," he growled, half-playful, half-serious.

Abby *didn't* tell him, though it was the truth. How many nights had she lain in bed thinking of him! Where would it end?

"I think you're just missing Alexandra," she teased.

"As you're missing Sean?"

"Touché."

And so the banter went. Every few minutes Ben called to Brian; every so often he crept to the edge of the ravine and looked down. Each time he returned to Abby, sodden but no worse for the wear.

Stranded, Brian went nowhere. The rain continued unabated. The air, though warmer than it had been on the mountaintop, cooled with the progression of the afternoon. Abby overlooked chilled legs and numb feet for the pleasure of curling up against Ben.

As one hour slowly ticked into two, then three, and the weather seemed if anything to worsen, they spent more time at the edge of the precipice, stretched out flat, doing their best to keep Brian's— and their own—spirits up. Abby heard stories of Ben's campus adventures; likewise, she shared the best of her examining room tales.

Tension inevitably mounted with the fading of daylight. Trying his best to hide his worry, Ben stole glances at his watch when he thought she wasn't looking. But she saw. Hadn't she begun to think the same thoughts? How much colder it would be soon, how much more difficult the rescue, how much more tedious the trek down? Hadn't she begun to shiver uncontrollably and to wonder whether her toes would ever be the same? Hadn't she begun to fear for Brian, whose exposure to the hostile elements had to be much worse than theirs?

When Ben's arms held her now, she felt his uneasiness. When his fingers tucked wet strands of her hair back under her hat, she knew of his anxiety. When he launched into renewed oaths of regret that she'd stayed, she had no choice but to hear his anger.

Finally, with the coming of darkness, help arrived. Indeed, the rescue was more difficult now. But with the aid of floodlights and cables, it was successfully accomplished, then celebrated with brandy-laced coffee before the long downward hike began.

By the time Abby finally crawled into bed shortly before midnight, she was chilled through and through. A hot bath had done little to warm her; memories of Ben's warmth faded quickly. When he knocked on the door, quietly opened it, and came to sit beside her on the bed, she was too occupied with controlling her shivering to analyze his presence.

"How do you feel?" he asked softly.

"Freezing." She burrowed lower beneath the quilt.

His hand moved gently against her cheek. "You feel warm."

"I'm *freezing.*"

"I mean *warm* warm. As in a fever."

"I'm fine."

"Have you taken anything?"

"No."

"Smart lady . . . for a nurse," he quipped sarcastically. Then he stood and headed toward the bathroom. "Have you any aspirin?"

"No."

He stopped in his tracks, then redirected them. "I've got some. I'll be right back." Within seconds he held a cup of water to her lips and insisted that she swallow the two white pills he'd produced. "That's better. Can I get you anything . . . some warm milk . . . brandy?"

"I've already had more than I can stomach." The Abbotts had plied her with food, and it had done nothing but make her queasy. "I think I'll just go to sleep."

"You're sure that there's nothing I can do?"

She managed a weak grin. "What's the matter, Ben? Feeling helpless again?"

"Damn it, yes! You never should have stayed up there with me. I knew it from the start! Now you're getting sick and since the state doesn't allow for time off—"

He'd said more than he'd planned. For the first time Abby opened her eyes wide. "I'll be dismissed!" she breathed unsteadily.

"Right."

It would all have been in vain? Never! "I'll be fine in the morning!" she declared. "You'll see."

She wasn't exactly fine . . . nor was she deathly ill. If she was paler than usual, her blusher would take care of that. If her bones ached, she could stay off her feet. If her cheeks were warm, there was no one to know. No one . . . except Ben.

He poked his head into her room on his way to run, took one look at her, went for more aspirin, and forbade her to move until he returned. She was more than happy to accede, having given up the idea of running the instant the phone had jarred her from a fevered sleep at six. The extra hour's rest was a must if she was to function that day.

And it *was* a must that she function that day. The defense opened its case with a startling revelation. Derek Bradley would *admit* to having abducted Greta Robinson, to having held her prisoner much as the prosecution had claimed. Rather, his not guilty plea would be based on the defender's intent to prove temporary insanity. Derek Bradley, obsessed by love, so his counsel declared, had been driven by an irresistible impulse to kidnap Greta Robinson that day so many months before.

Derek Bradley spent the better part of the week on the witness stand. With each day, tension in the courtroom mounted. An irresistible impulse. It was a legal term, an even more complex psychological term. Following the defendant's testimony was that of a team of psychiatrists, each flown in from outstanding medical establishments across the country, each supporting the premise that Derek Bradley had been compelled to do what he had done by the force of love. Abby's feelings were in utter upheaval by the time Friday arrived and the defense rested its case.

Having fully recovered from her experience on the mountain, she concentrated on understanding the arguments. But lines blurred, images were confused. She'd lie awake at night and think.

An irresistible impulse. What *was* it she felt for Ben, and why did she struggle so to keep herself from running to him? The voice of reason against the voice of impulse. And just as she was hard put to decide her feelings about Derek Bradley's guilt or innocence, she simply couldn't reconcile her own torment.

That Ben was enduring similar anguish alone in *his* room at night was something she could only surmise. As the week progressed, he too grew more troubled. His temper was shorter, his tone harder. She could see new furrows on his brow, deeper grooves by his mouth. Smiles were few and far between.

Abby had the agonizing sense of time running out. Monday and Tuesday would see the prosecution's rebuttal witnesses; then the judge would charge the jury. It was not unrealistic to guess that by Thursday the trial might be over.

And then what? Her eyes filled with tears each time she thought of it. *Then what?*

"Will Sean be coming on Sunday?"

She tore herself from the misery of her daydreams to face Ben with a start. "Excuse me?" She sat on the window seat in the living room. He'd come to stand over her.

"I asked if you'd invited Sean for Sunday." The judge had decided that, given the length of the trial and its peculiar emotional pressure, there would be a two-hour visiting period at the inn on Sunday afternoon. Ground rules had been established. Only family or, in the case of unattached jurors, one close friend could come. All would meet in the living room, with an extra detail of court officers assuring that there was no discussion of the case itself.

Abby stared at Ben. "Sean? Oh . . . Sunday." He looked so cold. She had to consider the future. "Yes . . . uh, yes. Sean will be coming."

"That's good," he grumbled, then turned and walked away leaving her unhappier than ever.

Yes, she would invite Sean, if only to protect herself from thoughts of Ben. And, of course, Alexandra would probably come.

It was an afternoon not to be forgotten. Dressed in a peasant skirt and blouse whose gathers and ruffles made her look all the more feminine, Abby went downstairs early to meet the families of those other jurors she'd come to know.

The atmosphere was as close to festive as anything in the past two and a half weeks had been. There were hearty embraces, smiles, and laughter, and everyone enjoyed a lavish cold buffet.

Conscientiously ignoring her own apprehension, Abby moved from one eager group to the next. Perhaps the air of merriment was a good omen, she mused. Then she stopped to look around for Ben. He hadn't come yet. Another good omen? Perhaps he hadn't invited Alexandra after all! Then why had she invited Sean? She wasn't *that* anxious to see him. . . .

Patsy, of course, had invited Bud. Her face beaming, she appeared at the door of the living room hand in hand with her handsome ski bum. Abby caught her breath and straightened, unable to take her eyes from him. Indeed he was as good looking as Patsy had claimed. He also looked terribly, terribly familiar. . . .

Slowly understanding dawned. By the time Patsy

and Bud reached her, Abby wore a smile of grudging admiration. "I don't believe it," she whispered, shaking her head in amazement that they'd pulled it off as smoothly as they had.

Patsy winked. "Abby, I'd like you to meet Bud. Bud, this is the friend I've told you about."

Bud extended his hand and grinned broadly. "How do, Abby?" Then he cocked his head and feigned puzzlement. "Say, haven't we met somewhere before?"

"Your guy's got all the right lines, Patsy," Abby said, laughing. "But is it Bud . . . or Peter?" It had taken her a minute to recognize him without his hiking gear. And, of course, those nights at the hunting lodge, then the movie theater . . . she hadn't been able to see his face at all.

"Peter, Jr., known all my life as Bud." The explanation was simple.

"Mountaineer, usher, waiter . . . you're a versatile guy."

"I think so." Patsy beamed as she linked her arm through her Bud's, and the two went in search of a corner in which to talk.

Abby was unaware of their departure, though, for Sean chose that moment to appear at the door. By his side was a stunningly attractive blonde. Ben's appearance moments later confirmed her identity. The afternoon went steadily downhill from there.

Abby hugged Sean, or was it the other way around? Ben hugged Alexandra, or was *it* the other way around? Introductions were made . . . and there they stood. All four of them. Chatting about the inn, the weather, the foliage, the World Series. Ben made no move to leave Abby with Sean; Abby had no intention of leaving Ben with Alexandra. As a foursome, they helped themselves to the spread put out by the Abbotts. As a foursome, they stood munching on the goodies. As a foursome, they greeted others who stopped for introductions.

Abby had little idea what she said, even less what was said by the others. She only knew that her face grew stiff from the smile she'd pasted there . . . and that Ben seemed to be enjoying himself tremendously. He and Alexandra *did* make a handsome couple, she had to admit, and Alexandra hadn't left Ben's side for a minute.

It was confusing and annoying, tiring and frustrating. She'd never felt as relieved as she did when the court officers quietly passed the word that it was time for the guests to leave. Sean lightly brushed Abby's cheek with a kiss; Ben did the same to Alexandra. Sean and Ben shook hands; Alexandra and Abby exchanged polite farewells. Finally, as they'd arrived by chance, so Sean and Alexandra left together.

Only then did Abby turn to glare at Ben.

eight

BEN GLARED RIGHT BACK. "WHAT'S THE MATter, Abby? Where's the smile now?"

"I was just wondering the same about you! For someone who made a point of claiming that your relationship was innocent, you certainly went out of your way to charm Alexandra." Her pulse raced on a surge of jealousy.

"Alexandra was glad to see me. A man needs that kind of encouragement every once in a while," he barked pointedly. Abby was too busy wallowing in her hurt to hear him.

"And you loved it! You *and* Sean. I didn't miss the way *he* looked at Alexandra."

The muscles in Ben's jaw began to work. "Who are you kidding? He didn't take his eyes off *you!* It's obvious where his mind was—"

The room seemed suddenly quiet. Though the others looked away diplomatically, they were obviously aware of the argument. Cursing under his breath, Ben grabbed Abby's hand.

"Let's get out of here," he gritted through clenched teeth and had her out of the living room before she could react.

When she did it was in anger. "Just what do you think you're doing?"

They reached the stairs and he started up. "Something that's long overdue," he growled.

"Ben, you're hurting me!" She tried to wrest her hand from his, but his fingers only tightened. When his pace increased, she had to run to keep up. "Ben!"

"It's about time we had this out. Your little game has gone far enough!"

"My game? What are you talking about?" They'd reached the second floor. Ben didn't stop.

"That teasing game you play, Abby. You've put me through hell for the past two weeks . . . and I've got a fair idea that you've done the same to your Sean for far longer than that!"

"*What* teasing game? Ben . . . !"

Her protest fell on deaf ears. At the third floor, she was propelled down the hall past her own room to his. He pulled her in behind him, then slammed the door and bolted it. Then he turned, leaned back against it, and slowly, slowly raked the full length of her body with his eyes. She knew what was on *his* mind.

"Ben. . . ." Slightly breathless from the upstairs dash, she pulled herself up straighter. "Let me go."

"No way, Abby. It's that moment of truth."

Her hair gently swirled about her shoulders when she shook her head. "No. You're upset. You don't know what you're doing."

He loosened his tie with an indolent hand and slowly pulled it off. "I know precisely what I'm doing . . . and it's about time." The tie fell to the carpet. He took a step forward and shrugged out of his blazer. That was easily tossed onto a nearby chair. Abby took a step backward.

"Please, Ben . . . let's talk. . . ."

"No! We've been that route before, and it leaves

me more frustrated than ever." He began to work on the buttons of his shirt. Abby's mouth went dry.

"Frustrated?" she whispered hoarsely. "Is that what this is about? *Your* frustration?"

"Why not? It seems I'm the only one to suffer from the problem. Not you. You're content with near misses. Well, Sean may not have been man enough to force your hand, but I am." He tugged his shirt-tails from his slacks. Soon the shirt hung completely open.

Abby swallowed hard. His chest was so broad, so beckoning. She'd only seen it from a distance, that day at the lodge. Now it was no more than an arm's length from her, lightly bronzed and with a tawny tee of hair that tapered alluringly into his slacks. She dug her nails into her palms.

"You're wrong," she gasped. "You were the one who walked out on me that night when I begged. . . ."

He slid the shirt from his shoulders, and it joined his blazer on the chair. "That was an aberration. It won't happen this time. I've had enough of looking at you, being near you, wanting you . . . and not having you. That's done." His hands went to his belt. He unbuckled it, then paused. Eyes wide, Abby stared, before forcing her gaze up to meet his. His eyes shone a rich silver hue, with a darker ring around their vibrant centers.

"What's the matter, Abby?" he taunted, a hard smile tilting his mouth. "No arguments? No pleas this time?"

She wanted him. Oh, how she wanted him. But not this way. Acting on reflex, she bolted for the door. Ben had only to reach out and snag her waist to stop her. He hauled her back against his body. "Oh, no, you don't. You could get away from Sean by being chosen for this jury. But you can't get away from me as easily."

"Ben . . . please . . ." She found her hands flattened on his chest and ached to explore his warm flesh. Her knees quivered, her insides fluttered. His nearness was everything she wanted . . . almost.

"Please what, babe?" he asked with the first hint of the tenderness she loved. Loved. Yes, loved. Without a doubt.

"Please . . . not in anger . . ." she whispered, feeling her body come alive under his hands as they skimmed the length of her spine. "Anything but that. . . ." Her fingers curled into the soft matting of hair on his chest.

Feeling the response of her body, Ben knew she wouldn't fight him. When he lowered his head and kissed her, her lips opened to him freely. She offered him the intimacy of her mouth, the liquid fire of her tongue, the sweet caress of her lips, destroying the last of his anger with the innocence of her giving. When at last he tore his lips from hers and drew back to look at her, there was that sadness she'd seen in him before.

"I can't promise you anything—"

"I know."

"And you'll stay with me?"

Forever . . . if only he'd have her. "Yes."

A vestige of wariness held his gaze steady. His voice was low and thick. "Then tell me what you want, Abby. Tell me now."

She should have reached the decision days ago, should have realized then that she loved him. Should have accepted it . . . even if he could not. It really didn't matter, did it? If she had these memories to hold with her . . .

Her fingers trembled when she lifted them to caress the muscular swell of his shoulders. "Make love to me, Ben," she whispered. "I want . . . you. . . ." Leaning forward, she pressed her lips to his chest.

She closed her eyes and savored his taste, running her mouth slowly across the matted surface that labored now with his breathing. Her hands moved likewise in exploration, eager to feel every inch of his hard, lean body.

With a low groan, he lifted her face and kissed her again, this time with a hunger that was fully shared. She ran her hands along the firm flesh of his back and found satisfaction in the flex of his muscles at her touch. But it wasn't enough. When his own hands began a restless wandering, she knew there was no going back.

His lips held hers in a mind-drugging kiss while she inched her way between their bodies and went to work on the buttons of her blouse. The backs of her hands brushed his torso; he sucked his breath in sharply. Then his fingers joined hers impatiently. Soon her blouse lay atop his shirt.

"Ahhh . . . babe," he moaned, pulling her against him. His arms pressed her closer, hands flattening on the base of her spine to remind her of their destination. She needed no such reminder. Her own body was afire, with the greatest heat centered opposite his.

Suddenly there was no time to waste. Ben unhooked her bra and peeled it off, then focused on the fastenings of her skirt while she picked up where he'd left off on his pants. If hands and legs collided with arms and bodies in the rush, neither Abby nor Ben cared. The only thing of importance was to be with each other . . . with nothing at all between them.

Then Ben's body was as bare as hers, and he swept her into his arms. Burying her face against his throat, she wrapped her arms tight around his neck while he carried her to the bed. He came down on top of her, reached back for her hands and pinned them to the quilt.

When he looked down at her then, despite everything he'd said, his eyes were luminous and loving. In them, she saw everything she wanted. It was the moment. Now. What she felt, this exquisite joy shooting through her body, was pure impulse, unsullied by that other world of justification and explanation. She no longer cared whether what she did was wise or right or practical. She only knew that she had to do it.

He inched his body intimately upward. When she arched in response, he smiled, then moaned. "Abby . . . Abby . . . I've waited so long. . . ."

The breadth of his shoulders dwarfed her own. His hips pressed hers to the bed. "I know," she whispered, driven wild by the sensation of his naked flesh on hers. "Hold me, Ben. Please hold me tight."

Releasing her hands, he slid his arms around her and lifted her from the bed. When he sat back on his haunches, her legs curved naturally around his hips and he slowly drew her down on him.

A long, gasping sigh slipped through her lips. She'd never felt anything as beautiful as that warm, hard life inside her now.

Ben's arms tightened convulsively. "That's it, babe. That's what I've been needing all these nights."

"Oh, Ben," she cried softly, "it feels so good."

A low groan of satisfaction, a deep animal sound, came from the back of his throat instants before he caught her lips in a kiss filled with all the promise he hadn't spoken. Then he slowly began to move her hips, and she cried out again at the intense joy she felt. The strength of it frightened her, as it had before. But now she surrendered herself to it.

Her breath came in short, jagged wisps as the fire raged hotter. His hands touched nothing but her hips; her arms wound tightly around his neck. With each thrust her body stroked his. Her breasts rubbed against him, growing swollen at the contact, their darkened peaks hard and full. Her belly slid warmly against his, her thighs moved over his in a rhythmic motion. And the pace quickened.

Then suddenly Ben could take no more. Backing her down to the bed, he thrust deeper, then again, sending her higher in turn until she cried his name once more, this time in disbelief as she neared the apex of unknown ecstasies. Her body was on the verge of bursting, her mind of disintegrating into a white-hot world of pleasure.

"It's all right, babe," he panted hoarsely. "Let it happen."

It happened with such force that Abby caught her breath on a ragged gasp. There was suspension, an explosion, then quake after quake of shuddering rapture. In the blinding glory, she never knew which spasms were her own and which Ben's. Her body throbbed endlessly. She struggled for breath. All she could think to do was to cling mindlessly to the man who'd brought her to this state.

Finally, inevitably, consciousness returned. Ben's body lay heavy on hers, his head fallen to her shoulder. Gradually his breathing and pulse rate returned to normal.

Abby lifted her hand to stroke the dampened skin of his back. Then, combing her fingers gently through his hair, she held him close. She'd never felt as fulfilled in her life as she did at that moment. Only two things could have possibly made her happier—being able to confess her love for him . . . and hearing him return the vow.

She eased her grip when he turned his head on the pillow. His forehead touched her temple, and she let her head fall closer. She felt his gaze, then met it.

"I'm sorry, babe. I couldn't wait any longer. Did I hurt you?"

"Of course not," she whispered back. *I love you.* "I wanted you, too."

Easing from her, he settled by her side, leaving one long, hair-shagged leg between hers in restful possession. He touched her cheek, then smoothed her hair from her brow. His fingers were strong, infinitely gentle. "I didn't mean all those things, Abby. I was upset."

"I know."

He kissed her lightly, sweetly, then relaxed his head against the pillow with a long sigh. The silence was a gentle epilogue to their passion. Abby listened to the evenness of his breathing close by her ear and wished she could stay right there forever. Eyes closed, she basked in a rare sense of bliss.

"Sean seemed like a pleasant enough fellow." Ben's voice was an intimate whisper.

"He is. . . . Ditto for Alexandra."

"I suppose. I don't know. . . . I don't think I heard a word she said."

Abby nudged him in the ribs. "You did so. You were entranced."

"The word is obsessed, and it wasn't with her. I was too busy concentrating on you . . . you and Sean."

"Jealous?"

"In a word."

"Well," she took a deep breath, "if it's any consolation, you weren't the only one."

"You mean Sean was jealous?"

"I mean *I* was jealous. Sean seemed oblivious to it all." Her brows knit. "As a matter of fact, he was very happy to take off with Alexandra at the end there." She turned her head to look at Ben. "Does that bother you?"

"He's welcome to her. I don't want her!"

So much for Abby's green-eyed imaginings. Then, for a moment, she pictured Sean and Alexandra together and chuckled. "That would be really funny . . . if they ended up going out after meeting here."

"Almost as funny as *our* meeting here," he murmured.

"Funny" wasn't one of the words she'd used in her soul searching. There had been "bizarre," "unreal," and "preposterous." Even now she couldn't quite understand her lying in bed with Ben. It made no sense at all to have fallen in love with him, much less to have given herself with such ardor.

A warm, wet stroking up the soft underside of her breast made her jump. "Oh!" She looked down in alarm to see Ben's tongue complete its journey. "You frightened me!"

"And who did you think it was?" He grinned as he shifted onto his side.

"I was . . . thinking about something else."

"So I noticed." His hand crept along her waist and began a lazy upward trek. "But that's against the rules."

"Which one?"

"No thinking out of court."

"That's *not* one of the rules."

"It is now. Let's call it Wyeth's Law." His fingers traced the roundness of her breast and brushed once across her nipple. The effect was instant. Abby gasped.

"What are you doing, Ben?" she whispered hoarsely.

His eyes followed the play of his fingers. "I didn't get a chance to see you before . . . it all happened so quickly." His hands moved over her then, exploring the soft curves of her side and hip before gliding back up across the silken skin of her stomach en route to her other breast. Even before it arrived, Abby felt herself swell in anticipation.

To her astonishment, that thirst she'd thought quenched was no longer so. Her body tingled back to warm, pulsing life. When he rubbed the pad of his thumb back and forth across her nipple, she moaned aloud. When he lowered his head to replace that thumb with his mouth, she strained closer.

He was right. Wyeth's Law. No thought allowed. Simply feel. Enjoy. Live.

Moving slowly upward, Ben left a trail of hot kisses along the slender line of her throat. His lips worshiped her eyes, her cheeks, the gentleness of her jaw, before finally reaching her mouth with a deep kiss.

But Abby's fingers itched. After all, she hadn't had a chance to see him either. When he released her lips with a thick moan of pleasure, she rolled to her side to face him. She'd touched his shoulders before. They were firm and as well developed as his chest. This too she'd touched. But his nipples. Flat as was so much of a man's body. She gently caressed them to hardness.

"What are *you* doing?" he growled softly.

"Same thing you are. I want to know, too."

"Know what?"

"What you feel like . . . all over. . . ."

Her hand felt his quick inhalation. But she was too entranced by the smooth skin of his side to linger. Her fingers explored the leanness of his waist, moved up the soft stretch to his armpit before lowering to his hip.

"I'm really not a tease," she whispered in belated response to an earlier accusation. "And I wasn't aware of playing a game." She moved her palm over

176

his thigh, finding its haired texture a distinct contrast to the smoother skin of his groin.

"Maybe not then," he warned unevenly, "but you're sure as hell playing one now."

She looked him in the eye, dead serious. "This is no game, Ben." *I love you.*

As though hearing the words she'd so carefully left unspoken, he too sobered. His eyes took on a fierce glow; his lips thinned. But if there were thoughts to be shared, he too opted out. Only a muffled oath betrayed his anguish.

"I can almost begin to sympathize with Bradley," he gritted. "If it's insanity we're talking about, he's not the only one with the problem. Maybe it's contagious."

"It is not."

"Then what's to explain what we're doing?"

Abby drew a pattern of invisible love signs from his stomach to his chest. *"You're* the one with the explanations. And the rules. What about Wyeth's Law?"

"Wyeth's Law." He cleared his throat while her hand worked its way lower again. "Right. Wyeth's Law." Then he took her lips in a kiss bound to eradicate all thought that dared intrude.

Once more there was only sensation. Hot. Fast. Throbbing. Ben's hands on her breasts, her stomach, then lower. Abby's own finding him, stroking him, building his need to a frenzied level. Her thighs parting, his fingers discovering her. Her writhing in a rush of emotion so great she thought she'd explode there and then.

But he held her off, drawing back at the last, teasing her mercilessly, almost in punishment. When his hands finally cupped her bottom and he brought her to him again, she relived that exquisite joy only he could offer.

Much, much later they collapsed against one another, their bodies slick with sweat and utterly spent. Protected still by a heady daze, they fell asleep in each other's arms, awakening to shower together and dress for dinner, returning immediately after to undress and make love again.

Neither tried to rationalize what was happening. Their lovemaking was divorced from all logic. Abby rode with it, yielding to the impulse that seemed so much stronger than reason. There would be time to think . . . later.

On Monday morning, the prosecution began its rebuttal, putting on a line of expert witnesses—its own psychiatrists—to refute the notion that Derek Bradley had been temporarily insane at the time of the kidnapping. The issues grew more and more complex; Abby wasn't sure what to believe.

She recalled that first day of the trial, when the prosecution had outlined its case and everything had seemed so simple. Everything. Now she had only to look at the defendant to remember the emotional testimony both for and against his case. Now she had only to steal a glance at Ben to remember the extent of her own emotional involvement.

As always, he sat with an air of composure, of intense concentration. Why then couldn't *she* concentrate? All it took was the slightest movement on his part—a leg, an arm, a hand—and she recalled the long, bare length of that leg hooked around her own, the warm, supportive strength of that arm beneath her head, the incredibly tender work of that hand as it brought her to a high pitch of sexual arousal.

She felt torn, fragmented, a woman of three faces. There was the Abby Barnes who sat in court as a member of the Bradley jury. There was the Abby Barnes who would soon be returning to her home, her job, her friends. And there was the Abby Barnes who spent each night now with Benjamin J. Wyeth.

Each night. Sunday night. Monday night. Tuesday night. Glorious hours of passion during which Abby refused to think of anything but the magnificent man with her, in her, beside her. Wyeth's Law was firmly in effect.

If there was a rise in tension, it was easily attributable to the trial. On Wednesday morning, closing arguments were heard. First came the defense with a recap of its case and a final emotional plea for the sympathy of the jurors. An irresistible impulse. Derek Bradley's behavior had been the result of an irresistible impulse; he'd temporarily lost control of his senses.

Then came the prosecution with a last-ditch effort to convince the jury of its case. Reason. Malicious intent. Revenge. Derek Bradley's abduction of Greta Robinson had been a conscious and premeditated act. He deserved to be punished. Society should be protected. Justice must be served.

It was mid-afternoon when the judge charged the jury. In that solemn voice of his, he reviewed the specifics of the charges and outlined the jury's options. This was the final step before deliberations would begin.

Abby had never felt as keyed up. The situation, even beyond her involvement with Ben, was an overwhelming one. The jury was now to find the defendant guilty . . . or not guilty. The lawyers had been heard, the witnesses had been heard, the judge had been heard. There was nothing to do but deliberate.

Abby's stomach churned at the sight of the court officers placing fourteen pieces of paper, each with a juror's name on it, in a drum. Two names would be chosen. Two alternates. Those two would be segregated from the others for the duration of the trial.

They would be kept in custody on the chance of one of the regulars becoming sick.

It was something she and Ben had discussed more than once, that awful possibility of being deprived of participation in the deliberations after having endured the entire trial with the others. And, of course, in Abby's case there was a fear that now eclipsed even that. Should she be chosen an alternate, her time with Ben would in effect be over. . . . But she wouldn't be chosen. She wouldn't.

She held her breath when the first name was read. Joan Storrs. A woman. The chances were better than even that the next would be a man. Her pulse gave a jolt. What if it were Ben?

The clerk reached once again into the drum and drew out a piece of paper. It wasn't Ben. It was . . .

Abigail Barnes? Was that her own name she'd heard? It just couldn't be. She wanted so very badly to stay with him. Disbelief held her immobile until Ben's warm hand covered hers. Round in dismay, her eyes met his. His own pain was obvious.

But the court officer was waiting to lead Abby from the courtroom. Tightening his fingers on hers, Ben cocked his head almost imperceptibly toward the door. Then he released her hand.

If the highest point in her life had been reached in Ben's arms, this had to be the lowest. She'd never know how she made it to her feet, then out of the jury box and to John's side. She felt as though everything she'd become in the past three weeks had suddenly shattered.

Taking the steps in a daze, she heard Joan ask where they were going. Back to the inn. While the others deliberated in the jury room. While Ben deliberated with the others. Ben . . .

It was over for her. Simply a matter of sitting it out until the final verdict was returned. An hour. A day.

Two. But she'd be separated from Ben during all that time . . . even to the extent of having to move her things to a spare room on the ground floor of the inn, far away from Ben and the others.

Her own deliberations began then as she relived the past three weeks. Three weeks. Had it been that long? In hindsight it seemed the days had flown. But Ben had been in the picture then. Now each minute dragged.

What was to happen? She'd often wondered, but pushed the thought aside. There was no more evading the issue. She loved Ben Wyeth as she'd loved no other man . . . and now they'd be going their separate ways. After all, he had no intention of falling in love.

Distraught, she sat in her room, unable to do anything but study her watch. How long would they deliberate? When would they return to the inn? Would the trial be over tonight? Tomorrow?

Dinner was a quiet affair with Joan, herself, and Grace, who'd replaced John with the alternates in deference to their gender. Abby was scarcely able to talk, much less eat. And those few things she did say reflected her thoughts.

"Won't they be back for dinner?" she asked Grace, all too aware of the empty dining room.

"They'll be eating at the courthouse."

"How long will they be allowed to go on tonight?"

"Possibly until nine or ten."

"Then what?"

"If they haven't reached a decision by then, the judge will suspend deliberations until morning."

"Is everyone else there . . . just sitting around the courtroom?"

"They're . . . within calling distance."

"And the verdict really could come in at any time?"

"It's possible. Not probable."

"Why not?"

"The trial's lasted three weeks. There's a lot of testimony to review . . . unless the jury reaches a decision on the first ballot."

"When might that be taken?"

"It may have been taken already."

If so, there had been no unanimous decision. For the drive leading to the inn was empty, the lobby deserted. There was no sign of jurors filing in to pack their bags and return home at last.

Home. Abby tried to envision her house and came up with the image of a lonely place. She tried to envision the office and came up with a place of necessity. She tried to envision Sean and drew a blank.

As the evening dragged on interminably, she grew more and more upset. The disbelief she'd felt in the courtroom had long since been replaced by feelings of loss and frustration, of anger, of misery. Try as she might to cope, she simply couldn't.

Nine o'clock came and went, as did ten. With tears ever on the brink, she never left her room. Instead she listened for the noise, any noise that would signal the return of the others. Of Ben.

But isolated as she was now, she heard nothing. Pacing the floor did nothing to ease her tension. Lying on the bed was worse. Showering, she could only recall those times she and Ben had stood beneath the warm spray together.

At long last, wearing the nightgown that had been unnecessary during the past few nights, she slumped down on the window seat and stared dully out at the pitch black night. There was nothing there, nothing to blur when her tears finally gathered in force and spilled in slow trickles down her cheeks.

It was well past midnight when the quiet turn of

the doorknob penetrated her wretchedness. Her head flew around; her heartbeat faltered. The door inched open and Ben stole through. For only a second, they stared at one another. Then she was in his arms, clinging to him, being held tightly.

"Oh, Ben," she sobbed, crying uncontrollably now.

His voice was not much steadier. "I know, babe. I know." He pressed her cheek to his chest and buried his face in her hair. "It's all right . . . all right."

She seemed to cry forever, unable to stem either the tears or the shivering of her body. At some point he lifted her and carried her to the bed, but she only knew that he stayed with her, and that was all that mattered.

Then finally, like a sedative, the warmth of his body calmed her. He caressed her back and her arms, drew her hair back from her face. Her tears slowed, her limbs gradually relaxed. And she met his lips in a kiss so fierce as to instantly activate Wyeth's Law.

Her nightgown slid from her body as though it hadn't belonged there at all. He undressed as quickly. And then he came to her, adoring her body as only he could do. Every part of her was his, and he gloried in the possession. He left no small spot untouched by his hands, his lips, his tongue.

She opened herself to him without restraint, expressing her love through total abandonment to his passion. His passion . . . her own . . . there was no distinction between the two. When he finally entered her, they were one as they'd been destined to be. Their union was the only thing that made sense.

Too fast it was ended. When Ben slid from her bed before dawn and dressed, she watched him in sorrow. Then, without a word, he took her in his arms for a silent goodbye, a last, heart-rending embrace. And he was gone.

If the day before had been a nightmare, Abby found this new one to be even more of an ordeal. Nothing had been resolved. Her torment continued.

She felt as if she were the one awaiting judgment, with the outcome a sadly forgone conclusion. Yes, Ben had come to her, but it hadn't proven anything other than that he'd understood her anguish, perhaps even needed solace of his own. After all, *he* was the one sharing the burden of judgment for that other trial, not Abby.

It hurt. Everything hurt. The trial . . . the prospect of returning home at any time . . . Ben. Especially Ben. He didn't want love, didn't want marriage. It would all be over soon.

The morning crept along through her silent misery. By afternoon she feared she couldn't take much more. Time was a knife twisting, twisting in her heart.

Then, late in the afternoon, word finally came. The jury had reached a decision. To Abby's surprise, even the alternates were expected to be in the courtroom when the verdict was read.

Heart pounding, she joined Grace and Joan for that short, final drive to the courthouse. Legs wobbly, she climbed to the second floor courtroom and passed through its large leather doors.

The tension within hit her like a gust of hot, stifling air. The room was filled to overflowing, its back walls lined with those who hadn't found seats. All waited uneasily for the jury, then the judges to take their places.

Abby was shown a seat just in front of the raised jury box. Looking toward the defendant, whose pallor reflected his own state of anxiety, she could almost sympathize with him. To fear that one's life was about to change drastically . . . and for the worse . . .

She swung around when the rear doors opened and the jury returned, single file, down the aisle. Their expressions were uniformly grave, their eyes straight ahead. That they'd been through their own form of hell was obvious.

Ben's face was drawn, his back straight. His eyes met hers for only an instant, telling her nothing but that he too had reached the end of a tautly held rope. Stomach knotting, she watched him move on to his place in the jury box.

Then the court officer banged her gavel, the courtroom stood, the judges returned, and everyone sat.

"Have you reached a verdict?"

The foreman, Bernie Langenbach, stood with a small piece of paper in his hand. "We have, your honor."

"Will the clerk of court please read the verdict."

The clerk stepped forward, took the paper from Bernie, and unfolded it. Abby held her breath.

"The defendant, Derek Bradley, is found . . . guilty."

Guilty. On both counts. Shaken by the implication of the finding, Abby looked sharply down. Would *she* have voted for guilty had she been part of that final process? Would she have agreed with the others that the defendant had acted on reason, as opposed to that irresistible impulse, as the defense had argued?

Once, the answer would have been simple. Human beings were creatures of reason. She was. Ben was. Yet . . . hadn't *they* acted on impulse, giving in to an irresistible impulse night after night?

Stunned, she barely heard the burst of noise in

185

the courtroom, much less the judge's dismissal. When Grace touched her arm and indicated that the jury would return to its room for a final time, she stood. The other thirteen had gone before her. It was over.

If she thought she'd cried herself out last night, she was wrong. To her dismay, her eyes again filled with tears. It took every bit of determination she possessed to hold them in check.

As though aware of her state, Grace kept a firm hold of her elbow. The courtroom had suddenly come alive, spectators now swarming restlessly toward the aisles, waiting only for the trial participants to clear the room before surging forward.

"Hold on, Abby," the court officer spoke kindly by her ear. "We're almost there."

They reached the doors, then worked their way down the winding stairs to arrive, moments later, at the jury room. When Grace suddenly vanished, Abby found herself alone.

This was where it had begun over three weeks before, where she'd seen Ben for the very first time. Then, she'd been composed, self-confident, in high spirits. Now she fought tears.

Where was he? She scanned the small groups of jurors. Ben wasn't there! Had he gone already? *Gone?*

"Abby!" He came on the run from behind to grab her arm and turn her. He was tense, unsmiling, and short of breath. "Marry me, Abby. I've just spoken to the judge. He'll do it now."

Her eyes widened. Her heart thundered loudly. Then, without so much as an instant's thought, she nodded.

nine

WITH THE POWER VESTED IN ME BY THE state of Vermont, I now pronounce you man and wife." Theodore Hammond slowly closed his book, looked directly at Ben, and nodded. When Ben did nothing, the judge raised one silvery brow and cleared his throat. Still no response. Then, eyeing the groom more indulgently, he cocked his head toward Abby. "You may kiss the bride now, Dr. Wyeth."

Only then did Ben come to life. "Uh . . . yes." Turning to Abby, he lowered his head and kissed her. Her lips were the only warm part of her body. He lingered, as caught in a trance as he'd been moments before. Abby, too, savored that instant. It seemed the only reality.

Then the judge cleared his throat again, and they broke apart in time to accept his handshake. "Congratulations to both of you. I must say that this is a new one for me." He looked from one to the other. "It'll make quite a story for the grandchildren." Then, for the first time, this man who'd given meaning to the phrase "sober as a judge" smiled. "Good luck to you."

They stood in the judge's lobby beyond the now-empty courtroom. Because of the unusual circumstances, the judge had waived the normal waiting period and consented to perform the ceremony there and then. It had been a brief exchange of vows, with Patsy and Brian serving as witnesses.

Now, as the judge stepped back, Brian shook hands with Ben while Patsy turned to hug Abby. "Congratulations, Abby! I knew it would work," she whispered gaily. "Be happy!"

Abby couldn't speak. She hadn't said a word since "I do," and very little before that. It had all happened so quickly that she was breathless. But her eyes were bright, and she managed a smile. Then, with a final squeeze for support, Patsy made way for Brian.

"Congratulations, Abby. You've got a good man."

Again, she could only smile and nod. When Ben's arm slipped around her waist, she was relieved. *Someone* had to take control, and she seemed totally helpless.

"Let's go, Abby. We've got lots to do."

It wasn't the most romantic thought, or the most comforting. It was, however, practical. The vans were waiting to take them for the final time back to the inn, where their fellow jurors joined in an impromptu celebration thrown by the Abbotts. There was champagne to toast the newlyweds, caviar and Brie to accompany it, and a huge cake with a sugar-scripted message of farewell for them all.

Bags were packed, final goodbyes said. Then Abby found herself in the back seat of a cab, alone with her husband. It was the first quiet moment they'd had together since the night before.

For several long seconds the cabbie seemed to be the only one capable of functioning, directing the cab down the drive to the main road while his passengers sat silently.

Then Ben let out a tired sigh. "It's hard to believe everything's over." He didn't look at her.

She felt as awkward as he seemed to. "Was it . . . terrible . . . reaching that verdict?"

"Bad enough." His mouth clamped shut. He obviously didn't want to discuss it.

"Where are we going first . . . your place or mine?"

His eyes remained glued to the dusk-shrouded scenery. "Mine. We owe ourselves a rest. Yours we'll save for tomorrow."

"News of the verdict will be all over the papers. I'll have to make some calls. Maybe I should . . . should plan to go in to work tomorrow?"

Ben looked at her for the first time. "No! I mean, take the day off. Hell, you were just married!"

Married? She couldn't quite believe it. Her mind felt numb. It was enough to anticipate returning to normal after a three weeks' hiatus. Normal was no more. That the world she returned to would be inexorably different from the one she'd left, she couldn't yet grasp.

"Are *you* taking tomorrow off?"

"I'll try," he said. She chose to attribute his curtness to fatigue.

"And Saturday?" He'd said he had classes on Saturday mornings. She had her own, for that matter.

"If I can." No promises either way.

No promises. Abby averted her gaze. There *had* been no promises made . . . even in spite of the vows they'd taken in the judge's chambers. What they'd done so impulsively had been simply to ensure that they'd stay together. For whatever his reasons, Ben hadn't wanted to let Abby slip from his life any more than she'd wanted it. But, just as he'd warned that first night they'd made love, he'd made no promises. And he now sat beside her, her husband, an unknown in many ways. The thought sent a ripple of apprehension through her.

"Are you all right?"

She turned toward him. "Uh-huh."

"You look pale."

"It's been a . . . a . . ." She couldn't find the right word. ". . . long day." That was one way of putting it. Totally understated. Not quite exact. But did she want to call her wedding day—her *wedding day?*—nightmarish? Or bizarre? Or basically nonsensical? Ben seemed tense enough on his own without having to deal with her overwrought emotions.

"What will you tell Sean?"

She caught her breath. "That I . . . I need another day's rest. He can do without me until Monday."

"I mean about *us.*"

Their gazes locked and she sensed a wariness in him. Anxious to ease it, she answered without hesitation. "That we're married." Hard as it was to believe, it was fact. And Sean of all people deserved to be told quickly. News must have already reached him that the trial was over; even now he was probably trying to reach her on the phone.

"He may give you a hard time."

"I can handle it . . . and besides, there's nothing he can do." It was done. She *was* Mrs. Benjamin J. Wyeth. Little by little, the enormity of it crept through her numbness, leaving her senses all ajangle.

"Are you sorry?" he asked, still cautious.

"Sorry? Of course not! I"—she caught herself just in time—"I . . . knew what I was doing." Barely . . . but that was secondary. The fact that she loved him covered for all the thought she *hadn't* given to their marriage.

"Will your family be shocked?"

"Probably. They'd given up on me."

He seemed to relax momentarily and actually permitted a half-smile. "Why would that be? You're not exactly . . ." he skimmed her length appreciatively, ". . . over the hill."

"No." Her own lips twitched. How much better she felt when he warmed to her! "But I've fought them whenever the subject has come up."

"Ahhhh. Your mother." He recalled an early argument they'd had beneath the oak at the inn.

She nodded. "My mother. Once the shock wears off, she'll be thrilled! . . . What about you?" Her voice took on a pert note of teasing. "What'll the reaction be on campus when word spreads that its bachelor professor is a bachelor no more?"

"There's bound to be a riot. All those coeds who wait after class for special assignments—"

"You're kidding me," she broke in.

"Well . . . maybe no riot."

"What about the *coeds?* You only talked about Alexandra. What's this about *coeds?*"

"Jealous?"

"Yes!" This was the man she loved!

Ben's eye caught the determined tilt of her chin. His smile faded, as did all sense of play. "You needn't be. I took that vow of loyalty today, too. I'll live up to it."

"I know you will," she said softly, believing it firmly. He'd be faithful; he was that kind of man. As for allowing himself to love her . . . that was something else. "Are *you* sorry, Ben?"

He didn't answer for a while, simply gripped the handrail and stared at the dimming roadway. Abby felt her palms grow clammy. Finally, he turned to look at her. "No, Abby. I'm not sorry."

But he said nothing more. She wanted to ask why he *had* married her, why the idea had come to him in the first place, but there was that small part of her that feared his answer. Better to leave well enough alone, she mused, shifting her gaze to the window.

Darkness had fallen since they'd left the inn. By the time they reached the outskirts of Quechee, there was little to see. At Ben's direction, the cab left the main road and traveled up a long private way before coming to a halt at the top of a rise.

Abby swallowed hard, realizing that this was *her* home now as well. As if sensing her apprehension, Ben helped her from the cab and kept her hand in his during the walk to the door.

The pale silver light of a demi-moon illuminated the outline of a modern home, more sprawling than tall, spreading silently to either side of its large front door. Even at first glance and in the dark, the house had the same clean-cut, casual air of its owner. Modern, but definitely Ivy League.

"Did you build it yourself?"

He opened the door and released her hand to let her walk in. Reaching to the side, he flipped on the lights. "I had it built for me, if that's what you mean. I had a pretty good idea of what I wanted and couldn't find it ready-made."

"I can see why!" she exclaimed, delighted by the way the foyer led into an open, semicircular living room off which the rest of the house branched. With tour-guide formality, Ben pointed to the left and the dining room, kitchen, and laundry, then to the right and the bedrooms, bathrooms, and studies. Straight ahead were sliding glass doors that opened to . . .

"A deck and patio," he meshed his words with her thoughts. "If the summer season were longer up here, I might have put in a pool. It's still possible. . . ." He shook his head slowly, his face a mask of momentary confusion. *"Anything's* possible. . . ." His voice trailed off, and he turned abruptly to retrieve their bags from the door. "Come on. I'll show you my . . . our room."

He led and she followed. They were husband and wife; one would never have guessed it. Except for momentary lapses, he was reserved, and she was uneasy. That they'd loved so wildly in each other's arms for the past four nights, that they'd shared such warm and tender times together seemed impossible.

Ben showed her to the bedroom and put their bags on the bed. He made room in the closet for those clothes she had with her, then turned to unpack his own things. When he was finished, he excused himself and disappeared.

Emotionally drained, Abby collapsed onto the bed. It was the first moment she'd had to herself since . . . since that afternoon, before the jury had come in. So much had happened! She simply couldn't assimilate it.

She was Ben's wife. His *wife!* He'd asked . . . she'd accepted. Just like that. By rights, she should be thrilled. Wasn't she now guaranteed a life with him? Wasn't that what she wanted?

Why, then, this terrible awkwardness between them? She loved Ben; she knew that. And she believed that Ben felt very strongly about her. But love? He wouldn't permit himself to love her. And he seemed unhappy. *That* was what bothered her most.

Restless despite her exhaustion, she rolled to her feet and went into the bathroom to freshen up. The past three weeks had weaned her from her own home in South Woodstock, yet the newness of this place startled her. She opened the medicine chest to see *his* things—his comb and brush, his razor, his shaving cream. She turned around to see *his* towels hanging in rich terry splendor on the racks. She looked at the large stall shower and the oversized tub adjacent to it. Which did *he* use? Which would he use with *her*? *Would* he shower or bathe with her as they'd done so daringly at the inn?

Turning back to the sink, Abby reached for her makeup and analyzed what repairs were needed. The mirror reflected the image of a young woman whose pale face and shadowed eyes betrayed the upheaval in her life during the past hours. Nothing could be done about the upheaval; the best she could do was to apply blusher to correct the pallor and put a touch of foundation under her eyes. It was a slight improvement.

Then she reached for her brush and worked through the thickness of her hair with long, even strokes, stopping only when it shone. Better.

Looking down, she tucked her silk blouse more neatly into the waistband of her soft wool skirt. Cream silk, loden wool. Not quite a wedding gown . . . but then, it didn't really matter. The end result had been the same.

With that one thought, the weight of what she'd done hit her again, nearly negating her attempts to appear composed. Her stomach churned; her hands shook. Was she really married to Ben? Was she really *married?* In her wildest dreams, she never would have imagined the possibility when she'd left her home to do jury duty. Married! To Ben! . . . Bizarre!

Still edgy, she left the bedroom. There were phone calls to be made. She desperately needed to feel in touch with reality. Perhaps when she shared the news with her family and friends, it would make more sense.

Ben sat behind his desk in a study diagonally down the hall from the bedroom. The chair was angled sideways, and he leaned far back in it, so lost in his thoughts that he didn't see Abby at first.

"Ben?" she called softly.

His head swung around. As quickly, he sat forward. "I'm sorry. Have you been standing there long?"

"No. I just thought . . . maybe I should contact my friends. They'll be worried when they find I'm not home."

He cleared his throat. "Uh . . . sure. There's a phone in the den. You can be comfortable there."

"The den?" She pointed to her left.

The faintest ghost of a smile crossed his lips. "The den." He pointed to her right.

"Sorry. It'll take a little while, I guess."

"You've got time."

All the time in the world. This was her home, where she'd be living from now on. Looking now at Ben, the thought wasn't quite as awesome. His gray gaze captured hers with an instant's warmth, and she felt that familiar melting sensation flow through her. Her husband . . . and she loved him. If only she could feel free to tell him that. But he might freeze as he'd done once before when she'd inadvertently used the word. Worse, he might get angry. How *that* would hurt!

Then Ben's expression cooled. "Your phone calls, Abby?" he prompted in calm dismissal.

Taking a deep breath, she snapped her gaze from his. Her half-whispered "Yes" was offered in turning as she started down the hall.

"Other way!" came the deep voice from the study.

She stopped short, grimaced, and reversed direction. "Right," she nodded, feeling foolish enough not to look up when she passed the study again. It was a definite relief when she sank into a chair in the den and took the phone onto her lap. Definite . . . but short lived.

"You're *what?*"

"I'm married, mother."

"But, Abigail, I thought you'd been serving on a jury all this time!"

"I was. He was on it too."

"He was on the jury? And you just . . . decided to get married?"

It sounded—it *was*—so ridiculously impulsive. "Yes."

"Abigail . . . ?"

"Three weeks together is a long time," Abby tried to reason. It didn't help that Ben suddenly materialized to lounge against the doorjamb with his arms crossed over his chest.

"It's nothing! How can you *possibly* learn everything about a man in three weeks?"

"Can one *ever* learn everything there is to know?" With her peripheral vision she saw Ben smirk. Chalk one up for Abby.

There was a long silence from the Illinois end of the line, then finally the question. "Who is he?"

"You'll like him, mother."

"Who *is* he?"

Abby looked straight at Ben. "His name is Benjamin Wyeth. He's a college professor."

"A college professor?" This on a note of definite pleasure. "That sounds good. How old is he?"

Abby frowned, then helplessly mouthed the question to Ben. "Thirty-nine," she announced in relay before mouthing a silent thank you back to Ben.

"That old? You're more than ten years younger!"

"It's all right, mother." Again she looked at Ben, this time trying not to smile. "He's in excellent shape for his age." Ben rolled his eyes skyward but couldn't contain the humor playing at the corners of his lips. She felt better already.

"But . . . ten years, Abigail?"

"Don't worry. I know what I'm doing."

"Do you? Do you love him?"

Abby looked down at the phone and toyed nervously with its cord. "Yes."

"And does he love you?"

It was bound to come. But, hell . . . everyone had to tell a little white lie once in a while. "Yes."

In the silence that ensued, Abby suffered pangs of guilt. She was sure that Ben knew exactly what she'd been asked, and he'd certainly heard her answer. That it was all for her mother's sake seemed irrelevant. She still couldn't get herself to look back up at her husband.

Her mother's voice was suddenly softer. "Are you happy, Abby? That's all I want, you know."

Abby's eyes filled with tears, her throat with its now-familiar tightness. She bent her head lower. "I know. And . . . I am."

"Then I'm pleased for you, sweetheart. I only wish I could have been there with you."

"It happened so quickly. . . ."

"Well, you'll just have to arrange to make a trip out here, the two of you. Then we'll throw the party I've been planning all these years!"

"Mother . . ." Abby teased, but she was still choked up.

"Wait until your brothers hear the news! You haven't called them yet, have you?"

"No. You're the first."

"Shall I call them for you?"

"Would you mind? I've got so many calls to make."

"Of course I wouldn't mind! That's the joy of being a mother. You wait. When you have your own, you'll understand."

Her own. Children. Now she did look at Ben. Did he want children? They'd never discussed it! There was *so much* they'd never discussed!

"Are you still there, Abigail?"

"I'm here."

"I love you, sweetheart."

"I love you, too, mom."

"Will you call me again soon and tell me more about him?"

"I will."

"Has he got a phone number?"

"Oh . . . yes. Got a pencil?" Reading carefully from the tab on the phone, Abby gave her mother the number. Then, feeling suddenly more melancholy and frighteningly close to tears again, she took a steadying breath. "I'll talk with you soon, mom."

"Okay, sweetheart. And . . . congratulations."

"Thanks. Bye-bye."

Ben straightened slowly from the doorjamb. "Everything all right?"

Abby sniffed and brushed at her eyes with a forefinger. "Fine. She was pleased. I knew she would be."

"I'm glad. Perhaps we could take a trip out for one of the holidays."

"Could we?" Abby looked up more brightly.

"Of course. . . . You seem surprised. Did you think I'd keep you a prisoner on my mountain?"

She completely missed his humor. "I don't really know what to expect. Everything's happened so fast."

Ben crossed the room to stand before her. "I do want you to be happy, Abby. You know that, don't you?"

She wanted desperately to know it. "Yes."

"Then come." He held out his hand. "As your husband, I say it's time to eat. It's nearly nine. And if *you're* not hungry, *I* am."

"Dinner!" Taking his hand, she let him draw her up. "I've completely lost track of the time!" She'd make her calls another time. Now she had a responsibility to her husband. "Have you got anything in the house? I could fix up—"

Ben took her shoulders. "It's our wedding day, Abby. I think we can splurge and go out to eat." He grinned. "You deserve a break from the kitchen."

She didn't bother to answer. For one thing, he knew as well as she that *neither* of them had been in a kitchen for over three weeks. For another, her throat had tightened again. In that moment he was happy . . . if only it could last.

But it seemed too much to ask. As if in reaction to her warmth, he cooled. Rather than kissing her as he would have done yesterday or the day before, he took a deep breath and stepped back. An even-toned "Let's go," was all he said before turning on his heel to get the keys to his car.

A deep burgundy Audi took them to the restaurant. They ate and drank their fill. Then they returned. During the entire time, conversation was stilted. If Abby had hoped to be able to make Ben happy, she was initially, at least, a failure. He was distant, withdrawn. In turn, she remained quiet.

It was an inauspicious wedding feast, made all the more ominous by the strident jangle of the phone the instant they stepped—separately—over the threshold.

Moving quickly, as if glad to escape, Ben answered it in the den. "Hello! . . . Speaking . . ." He shot a glance at Abby, who'd come more slowly to the door. "Yes, doctor. She's here. . . . I believe that's *her* business." His voice was dead calm. "It's no 'cock-and-bull' story. It's true. . . . Now, just a minute. It's nearly eleven-thirty. She'll speak with you in the morning—"

"I'd better take it," Abby said softly, coming from behind to reach for the phone.

Ben muffled the receiver against his chest. "Are you sure? He's angry. I don't want you upset."

"I should have called him earlier. I owe it to him." She held out her hand, her eyes on Ben. He hesitated for a minute, then slowly passed her the receiver.

"Sean?"

"Abby! What in the devil's going on? I got word that the verdict had come in before five and I've been trying the house all evening. I assumed you were out celebrating with the other jurors. Now I hear a human interest story on the eleven o'clock news—a sideline to the trial claiming that you and Wyeth were married right there by the judge this afternoon. Abby . . . ?"

"It is true, Sean. I . . . I was going to call you earlier but things have been . . . overwhelming."

"I'll bet they have!"

Ben was right; he *was* angry. More probably hurt . . . it was only natural. "Please, Sean. Try to understand."

"Three lousy weeks! I've been working for *months!*"

"It just wasn't there between us. I told you that all along."

"And it's there with him?"

"Yes," she answered softly.

Sean paused, then swore more quietly. "Damn! I knew there was something odd between you two last Sunday. You wouldn't look at each other—but you wouldn't move away. Alexandra mentioned it, too. Fool that I was, I laughed it off. You were jury members, for God's sake! . . . Damn!"

"There's nothing you could have done, Sean. It just . . . happened."

"Things don't just *happen*, Abby. You *make* them happen. No one told you to get married today. Why on earth *did* you?"

That same question. The answer was simple. *Because I love him.* But Ben now stood by the window, in easy earshot of everything she said. "I wanted to."

"And you didn't want to marry me?"

I didn't love you! "It's not that simple."

"You love him."

"Yes."

The line was quiet for a longer time now, the silence finally broken by a sigh of resignation. "I guess that's it then."

"Yes."

"Will you . . . will you continue to work here?"

"Yes!"

Again he paused before speaking. "So he'll leave me that tiny part of you?"

"Of course, he will," she half whispered, finding her emotions deeply stirred once more. "And just because I'm married doesn't mean that I'm any less fond of you. It *will* mean that you'll be forced to go out and find someone who's *right* for you. That's all."

"Will you be happy, Abby?"

First Patsy, then her mother, now Sean. Happiness. The bottom line. A huge question mark.

"I hope so, Sean. I hope so."

Sean cleared his throat. "Then as your boss—or one of them—I'm giving you tomorrow off. Do you want next week too?"

"Oh, no! I don't think so!" Ben had said nothing of a honeymoon.

"So I'll see you on Monday?"

"Bright and early."

"Okay, Abby. Have a good weekend. Oh . . . and try not to worry about me. I've got a great bottle of ten-year-old Scotch waiting." He was the little boy again, only half jesting, but endearing nonetheless.

"Save it for your day. It'll come."

He snorted. "I think I'll give Alexandra a call. She

said she was going to plan a welcome home party for Ben."

"When did she tell you that?"

"I've spoken with her once or twice since last Sunday. We've been commiserating with each other. Now we've *really* got something to commiserate about!"

Abby's smile faded when she caught sight of Ben. He stared at her almost angrily. "Then give her a call, Sean," she offered quickly. "It might be fun."

"I'll think about it. . . . Monday then?"

"Monday."

"So long."

There was a finality about the click at the other end of the line that kept her own hand suspended for a second longer. Then she replaced the receiver and settled gently into the chair. "Sean said that Alexandra was planning something for you. Have . . . have you called her?"

But Ben didn't hear her. "Is it over?"

"Wh-what?"

"Your . . . thing . . . with Hennessy. Is it over for good? Did he accept the fact that you're married?"

"Of course he accepted it. He had no choice. But there really wasn't anything there before . . . not on my part, at least. I've told you that."

"I know." His eyes held hers steadily. "But your voice a minute ago . . . it sounded almost . . . regretful."

"I *am* sorry that Sean is hurt. I never meant that. But what about Alexandra? Did you hear what I—"

"I called her while you were unpacking."

"How did she take it?"

He shifted his gaze to the rug. "She was upset at first. Hurt also. But she accepted it. Much as with Sean, she had no choice."

And that settled that. One of the things that had

first brought Abby and Ben together had been the presence of nagging love interests on the outside. Now those love interests had been terminated. Their marriage had seen to that. It only remained for them to see to their marriage.

Sighing, Ben rubbed the back of his neck. "Look, I want to make a few notes. Why don't you take a shower and go to bed. I won't be long."

"Is this for your book?" she asked brightly.

"No. My classes." End of conversation. He walked to the door and turned toward his study. "Can you find everything you need?" he asked, pausing on the threshold without turning back.

She could barely hide her disappointment. Not only did he not want to discuss his work, but he was apparently bent on doing it, wedding night or no. "Yes. I can manage."

He nodded, patted the doorjamb once and left. Abby stared at the empty doorway. He was running. Still running. He simply didn't want to be involved. *Why then had he married her?*

As many times as she asked herself the question, she came up empty handed. Without a doubt, she was exhausted. Taking his suggestion, she showered and climbed into bed.

His bed . . . as large as that they'd shared at the inn, but infinitely more lonely without Ben. The ache of loving him was no proper company. She wanted *him.* Even now, lying alone in his bed, her body began to tingle at the thought of his lean, muscular body. At that moment she wanted nothing more than to run her fingers through his tawny hair and hold his head close for her kiss. She wanted nothing more than to mold her hands to his shoulders, then his hips.

This was her wedding night . . . and it was as bizarre as the entire affair had been. Had she made the right decision in marrying Ben? Had she made *any* decision . . . or had she simply acted on impulse?

Tossing to her right, she studied the wall, the window, the artwork. Tossing to her left, she studied the expanse of built-in closets and drawers. Settling onto her back, she studied the high stucco ceiling.

Frustrated, she threw the covers back and padded barefoot to the door, then down the hall to the study. "Ben?" He sat at his desk, his brow furrowed, his fists clenched one inside the other. "Ben?" He looked up in alarm, his features taut. "Why don't you come to bed," she urged him gently.

He stared at her as though she were an imposter, and she wished only that she'd stayed in bed. It hurt so when he looked at her in that angry, almost condemning way. Was it her fault that she'd fallen in love with him?

Her bewilderment must have gotten through to him, for he softened suddenly and stood, walking around the desk, entranced in a new way. When he finally stood before her, he lowered his gaze in slow appreciation of the woman who was now his wife.

Abby stood proudly, her heart hammering in her chest, while he took in the slenderness of her neck and the shapeliness of her shoulders. Then his eyes touched the top lace of her nightgown and slid lower to the firm outline of her breasts, the flatness of her stomach, the gentle curve of her hips.

It was all she could do to keep her knees from buckling, his heat had hit her that quickly. She'd always want him this way, she knew . . . then she also knew something else. If her body was the strongest lure she had, she'd use it for everything it was worth.

Without taking her eyes from his face, she reached up and slowly slid the thin straps of silk from her shoulders. Pulse racing, she eased her arms from them and let the fabric fall to her waist. Then, swallowing once, she shimmied the gown over her hips and let it fall to the floor.

Naked now, she waited for Ben to react. His breathing had grown more ragged, his gaze more hungry. But he didn't move.

When she could take the suspense no longer, she covered the inches between them, put her hands palm down on his chest, then slid them seductively toward his neck.

"I need you, Ben. I need you now. Please . . . come to bed with me."

For a final second he fought his desire. Then, with a low groan, he took her in his arms, lifted her and headed for the bedroom. No words passed between them when he laid her down, nor when he quickly shed his clothes. He murmured her name once before he kissed her . . . then words were unnecessary. Soft caresses and tender strokings yielded to more frenzied movements. At the apex of their passion they clung fiercely to one another . . . until their ecstasy became memory and they slid slowly, reluctantly back to earth.

Then the events of the day took their toll. Within minutes they slept. When Abby awoke in the morning, she was alone.

The week that followed was one of excruciating highs and lows. It began with the terse note she found on his pillow that Friday morning. "Have gone to work. Will be back by one." After the night's passion, her disappointment was intense. But one o'-clock saw him coming through the door, taking her back to her house for more of her things, then shopping. The bright gold band he placed on her finger was some encouragement, as was the fact that he chose a matching one for himself. That they walked on egg shells in each other's presence was a constant agony to her; that their lovemaking that night was as ardent as ever momentarily encouraged her.

But the next morning found him back off to the campus with no more than a clipped goodbye. Her only solace was the fact that, in a fit of frustration the morning before, she'd called and arranged to take over her own class again.

It was a brief respite from her torment. For she spent Saturday afternoon, then Sunday at home with Ben. He worked constantly in his study; she busied herself calling friends and writing notes. Only at night did he open to her like the man with whom she'd fallen so deeply in love.

In spite of her every attempt to alter it, a pattern emerged. During the day Ben was tense and distant, hardly concerned with what she did, going about his own life as he must have done before their marriage. At night he never failed to come to her, giving, if only in passing, the warmth she so badly craved.

The days were torture, the evenings bliss. Even Abby's return to work on Monday seemed to complicate things. For everyone wanted to know about Ben. Who was he? What did he look like? Had she *really* met him on the jury? Just when had they fallen in love?

It seemed unanimous. Abby's marriage to Ben had to be the most breathtakingly romantic event the county had seen in years. It was the talk of the office, not to mention her neighborhood. Even Sean rose to the occasion and joined in a spontaneous luncheon celebration for the new bride.

As for the bride herself, she simply smiled and nodded, accepting good wishes and congratulations as enthusiastically as she could. But the effort to conceal her anguish took its toll as the week went on, leaving her on edge more often than not.

Her mind was constantly on Ben and the gamut of questions she'd been asking herself for days. She grew dizzy wondering whether she'd been right in marrying him, whether she could ever make him happy, whether she could ever make him love her. It seemed the only pleasure they found was in those dark hours when all thought was suspended and pure passion ruled their lives.

Wyeth's Law . . . it had been amusing at one point. Now it gnawed at her endlessly. Logic versus need, reason versus impulse. On the one hand was the fact that Ben refused to love her, on the other the fact that they came alive in each other's arms each night. More and more, she yearned to love him freely. More and more, she yearned for his love.

When the weekend offered more of the same heartache, she began to despair. Ben looked more tired, tenser than ever. She knew she looked no better. When Patsy called her at work on Monday morning on the chance they might meet for lunch, Abby jumped at the opportunity. Patsy, with her spunk and her free spirit, might be just the one to give her a boost.

"Remember what I said before, Abby. You've got to break the rules every once in a while."

"What do you mean?"

"I mean," she said gently, "that you may have to *do* something. You're letting things fall into a routine that may kill your marriage if it doesn't kill you first. You look awful!"

"But what can I do? I'm afraid to say anything for fear of making things worse. As it is, he seems so angry at times. Maybe I'm just all wrong for him!"

"Abby, you couldn't be all wrong for anyone! And as for Ben, you'll just have to find a way to break through that wall of his. But don't wait too long . . . for your own sake. Please?"

But whereas Patsy might have done something that very same day, Abby was paralyzed. She loved Ben, she wanted him. The thought of confronting him tore at her mercilessly. Perhaps if she let it go another day, or two, or three, things might improve.

They didn't. Come Friday morning when Ben calmly packed his bags and announced that he'd be gone that night to a conference in New York, she knew she had to do something. They'd been married for two weeks. He might have easily taken her with him, had he wanted her company. But aside from their sharing a blind, nightly passion, they were virtual strangers. She simply couldn't endure that kind of relationship.

She spent hours on the note, writing and rewriting, choosing her words as though her life depended on it . . . which it did. For Ben *was* her life. Leaving him was going to be the hardest thing she'd ever done.

ten

"DEAR BEN," SHE'D WRITTEN, "IT SEEMS TOtally wrong to be putting this on paper rather than speaking to you in person. But you raced off to New York so quickly this morning . . . and then, you knew I was a coward.

"The last five weeks have been unreal for me . . . with first the trial, then our marriage. Things have happened too quickly. I need time to take it all in.

"I've gone to spend the weekend in my own place. Maybe there, where things are old and familiar, I can make some sense out of my life . . . out of our lives.

"I only know one thing . . . how much I love you. I have for a long time now . . . but then, you knew that, too, didn't you? I try to understand that you were hurt once, that you didn't want love *or* marriage again. But it's been harder and harder for me to remember that, when I need you so badly myself.

"The past week has been an agony for me . . . worrying every minute that I'll do or say something to anger you. I fell in love with a man who was bright and fun-loving, whose sense of humor could ease me over any tough situation. Where is he now, Ben? Is he *that* unhappy?

"Maybe you need time, too . . . to decide whether you made a mistake in marrying me. We rushed. It was an impulsive thing to do. But then, we've been doing impulsive things for weeks.

"I want to make you happy, just as I want to *be* happy. If the past two weeks have been any indication though, I'm not sure that's possible. At some point we have to stop and *reasonably* consider what we've done. That's what I'm going to try to do now.

"I do love you. Please remember that." She'd signed it simply, "Abby."

The letter was indelibly etched in her mind. She reread it during the drive to South Woodstock on Friday evening, then again repeatedly on Saturday while she puttered around her house, cleaning, neatening, sorting through things. Funny, Ben had made no mention of her selling the house, even on that first day when he'd taken her to pick up her things. Perhaps he had wanted her to keep it as the escape valve it now was. Lucky thing . . . but sad. Had he had that little faith in their marriage?

Distracted, she weeded through the summer clothes she'd left behind. Some went in a pile to discard. Others went directly into the wash. Then she attacked closets that had been neglected for months, kitchen cabinets, basement shelves. She worked Saturday night until she was worn out, then changed her clothes, strapped on her portable cassette player, and forced herself out to run.

She'd purposely avoided the light of day when neighbors might see her and ask her to stop. The last thing she wanted was conversation. It was hard enough coping with the well-intended enthusiasm she found daily at the medical center. But here . . . she needed solitude.

The night respected her privacy, asking no questions, offering no advice. She ran hard and thought hard, pushing herself to the limit. By the time she returned to the house though, she was nowhere near knowing what to do about the unhappy situation she'd made for herself. Ben *must* have already found her note. . . .

Fortunately she was too exhausted to do anything but strip, shower, and tumble into bed. It was at four in the morning, when she awoke wide-eyed once more, that the tears came.

He hadn't even called. Surely he was home . . . but he hadn't even called! Her note had been explicit as to her destination, and still he hadn't called!

The hours passed slowly. Dawn came. She dozed between bouts of crying and remorse. She should have stayed. Being with him under *any* conditions would be better than . . . *this!* But no . . . she'd been miserable the other way. Something *had* to be done. If only she could be sure she'd done the right thing!

Sunday morning . . . noon . . . mid-afternoon . . . nothing. No call on Ben's part, no miraculous brainstorm on hers. She felt every bit as distraught as she had at the end of the trial, when she'd thought for sure that her relationship with Ben was over. Was it now? Had it been inevitable all along?

Thinking back to past discussions, she wondered how she'd been so blind. There had been that time, at the very start, when they'd bandied about the merits of her marrying Sean. Ben had asked whether love was necessary, whether security, kids, sex mightn't be enough. Evidently, for him, it was.

Then later, when they'd talked of Alexandra, he'd been vehemently against remarrying. Why *had* he? Perhaps they'd have been better off had he stuck to his guns.

Time crept with agonizing slowness. The longer the phone remained silent, the more despondent

Abby grew. By the time the late afternoon shadows had faded to dusk, she saw it all clearly. She'd behaved impulsively . . . and now suffered for it. She'd shut her eyes to reality . . . and now paid the price. Buried in a world of his own, Benjamin Wyeth was simply not available . . . not for steady companionship, not for marriage, not for loving.

Suddenly uncaring of who saw her, she threw on her running suit, grabbed her cassette player, and took off. It was no different, she told herself, from any other day she'd run—even in spite of the gold band that gleamed on her finger and the tears that spiked her lashes. It was no different, no different at all. She still had her house, her friends, her job. She'd just have to adjust to the idea that she couldn't have Ben.

Unwilling to listen any longer to her thoughts, she fit the headset more snugly over her ears and turned up the volume of the recorder. Down one long street then right onto another, she barely saw what she passed. If a six-minute mile was her usual, she did well below that now, pounding the pavement with a steady slap of rubber that spoke loudly of her anguish.

Her vision blurred. She ran on. It was that twilight time, not day, not night, an eerie time . . . but she was too preoccupied to notice. Only when her back began to ache did she pause, and then for just a minute before resuming the pace. More than anything she sought utter oblivion.

When a car swerved to the curb just ahead of her, she barely saw it. When Ben stepped directly into her path, though, she couldn't miss him. Nor could she miss his anger . . . and that was *before* he tore the headset from her ears.

"Come on, Abby," he growled, grabbing her arm and pulling her toward the car. "Get in."

But Abby was filled with an anger of her own. Ben had been the one to propose their marriage, even knowing that he wouldn't give her what she needed. It had been all *his* fault!

"Let go of me," she struggled. "I'm running."

"You've been running for the last hour while I've been sitting back at your house half out of my mind with worry." His eyes had a bleak look that even dusk couldn't hide. "Now get in the car."

She tried to free her arm but he held it tighter. "I'm not going anywhere with you!"

"You're my wife," he growled as he clamped his other arm around her waist and propelled her toward his open door. "You'll come." A car approached from behind and passed without so much as a pause, its driver apparently assuming the quarrel to be a domestic one . . . which it was. Ben's point was made. Abby *was* his wife. She owed it to him—and herself—to see what he had to say.

At his gruff urging, she ducked into the car and slid behind the steering wheel to the passenger's side. Then she jammed her fist against her lips and stared out the window while Ben sped off. Thoroughly vexed, she paid no heed to the road, assuming that he'd take her back to her house to clean up. She was tired and sweaty, her hair a tangled mess. When the car turned from the main road and started up a familiar path, she straightened. Then, when the inn came into sight, her gaze flew to Ben.

"What are we doing here?"

He didn't answer until he'd swung the car around and parked. "It's time we got a few things straightened out . . . and what better place than the scene of the crime."

"Not funny," she declared but was relieved at least that his tone had softened. "But I can't go in there looking like this. It's not seven in the morning, and from the looks of these other cars the place must be filled with guests."

"You'll do." He was out the door and on his way to get her.

With a quick tug at her own door, Abby climbed out of the car. She didn't want his help. Ben took her arm nonetheless.

"I won't run away," she snapped.

"You did once."

"And what do you think *you've* been doing?"

Halfway up the path now, he looked down at her. "That's one of the things we've got to discuss."

She had to be satisfied with his word, for he offered nothing more. They passed through the door and crossed the lobby to the main desk, where Ben simply held out his hand to the clerk, took the key he was given, and guided Abby up the stairs. One flight, then the second, then down the hall to the room that had been his for the length of the trial, the room in which they'd spent such joyful, passion-filled nights.

With the closing of the door, they were alone. Again. Still. Abby moved to the window where she stood in an attitude of defeat.

"You planned this perfectly. Same room. Key waiting."

He shrugged. "All it took was a phone call. The room happened to be free."

In the light for the first time, she saw how tired he was. Even his stance had none of its usual zip. She ached to reach out, to breach that invisible barrier and soothe him. "How did . . . things go in New York?"

"Okay."

"When did you get back?"

"Last night."

No call then; terse answers now. Her sympathy could only go so far, when she was in such need her-

self. He'd abducted her and brought her here. Let
him talk.

It seemed forever that they stared at one another,
silently, warily. But the time couldn't have better
served Ben's purpose had he planned it. For against
her will Abby's anger slowly faded, fallen victim to
the one emotion that ruled her heart. It would take
far more than a few days' separation, far more than
bouts of anger and frustration to change the fact
that she loved Ben deeply.

"I missed you, Abby." His voice was low, raw. She
wanted to crumble but held her stance deter-
minedly. "I thought of you the entire time . . . then to
come home and find you'd gone . . ."

Oh, yes, there was pain in his eyes. Was that his
pain—or her own—that scissored through her? Was
there a difference?

As if not knowing what else to do, he dug both
hands into the pockets of his slacks and took a step
forward. Then he sighed, yanked one hand out again
and raked it through his hair. Abby hadn't moved.

"You know what your problem is?" he asked.
Startled, she shook her head. He went quickly on.
"You're too kind and loving a person. You don't
push me. And I take advantage of that."

It was beginning to sound ominously like a farewell speech. Abby felt her insides begin to twist un-
comfortably. But he was right. One part of her knew
it. And it wouldn't help to make things easier for him
now. She wrapped her arms around her middle and
bit her lip to keep from speaking out.

Ben walked to the dresser, then turned. "From
the start, I knew you'd be trouble for me. I felt too
strongly about you, even back then. But I couldn't
stay away. I tried to treat you like any of the other
women I've known over the years . . . but you're just
not casual affair material."

His gaze fell to the bed in remembrance, then low-ered to the floor as he struggled to express himself. He frowned, winced, then finally looked up. "You were right . . . what you said in your letter, Abby. I was hurt once. When Lynn died. I never wanted to live through that kind of pain again. It seemed safest not to get involved. . . . Then you came along and I *was* involved. But being frightened, I couldn't accept it. So I tried to keep you at arm's length."

Slowly he moved closer and she caught her breath. His eyes held hers now and were as clear a silver as she'd ever seen. "There was only one prob-lem, one little kink in my plan." His voice lowered to a smooth, caressing tone. "I'd fallen in love with you somewhere along the way. Keeping you at arm's length was pure hell."

Abby's heart skipped a beat. "I know," she whis-pered.

"You did, didn't you." His shoulders straight-ened, and he seemed just that bit less tired. More like himself . . . with a definite hint of vibrancy.

In response, she felt her blood warm and, without the need to protect herself, let her arms fall to her sides. "At night, when we were together, you were . . . loving. There's no other way to describe it. The daytimes . . . those were different. I'd figured out enough of the problem to try to be understanding, but after a while I just couldn't take it. That's why I left Friday, Ben. I didn't know how to get through to you."

His lips curved crookedly. "You certainly found an effective way."

"By leaving you? I did that for *me!*"

"But it worked." Closing the last steps between them, Ben touched her shoulders tentatively, then more confidently slid his hands down her back and brought her against him. Her arms curved naturally around his waist. "It suddenly hit me that I'd driven you away myself, that while Lynn was taken from me through no fault of my own, *I* was going to be fully responsible for losing you."

"You haven't lost me!"

"Not yet. But when I came home yesterday and found your note, I knew I was halfway there." Fully sober, he studied her features. "I was terrified. You can't believe the pain. It was as if it had happened all over again."

"But you didn't call. I kept waiting, hoping. You've been home for a full twenty-four hours!"

A sneer of self-disdain thinned his lips. "For the first time in my life I couldn't move. I couldn't do anything. Even after . . . after Lynn died, there were arrangements to make, things to be taken care of. But this time I was in a kind of limbo. One part of me kept thinking it would pass, that I could forget you, that I could live as I did before I met you. But everywhere I went I saw you, felt you, damn it, even smelled you!" He sucked in his breath. Only when he'd calmed did he speak again. "I need you, Abby, in more ways than one. I just can't live a nighttime existence; I want you in the day as well!"

"I'm here," she murmured, tightening her grip on him. Like her eyes, her heart was filled to brimming.

When he hugged her then, she thought her lungs would burst. "I do love you, babe. You have no idea how much!"

"*You* have no idea how much I've wanted to hear you say that!"

Their bodies swayed while he held her fiercely. "I love you," he said it again, then again. His lips were against her hair, but nothing could muffle the sound of his words. "I love you."

This time Abby's tears were of happiness. When Ben held her back, she mopped her cheeks. "I think

I've cried more in the past few weeks than I have in half a lifetime!"

"We'll just have to do something about that," he whispered. Then he kissed her with all the love he felt and she immersed herself in him.

When he released her lips at last, she gasped. "I forget everything when you do that."

"Oh-ho, no. No forgetting. This time we're doing it right, with our eyes open the whole way." He pressed warm kisses to her cheek. "I love you, Abigail Barnes. Will you be my wife?"

"We're already married!" she prompted in a stage whisper.

"Come on. Where's your imagination? . . . Will you?"

Here was the sense of humor she loved. She cleared her throat. "Well, now . . . I don't kn—"

A sharp squeeze to her middle cut off her breath. "Hmmm?"

"Yes."

"Right now?"

She looked down with a grimace. "Ben, look at me! I mean, the first time was bad enough. But . . . a sweaty running suit and sneakers?"

"You're right. We'll have to do something about that." His voice was hoarse; there was no doubt as to what he had in mind. He went to work on the zipper of her top. "Now I'm going to slide this down—like this—and then—here, move your arm a little, now the other—slip it off." The top fell to the floor. "Then I'm going to unsnap—where in the hell's the snap?" He leaned sideways. "There it is. Unsnapped and open." He shimmied her pants over her hips and knelt to pull them down.

"What is this . . . you're writing a manual now?"

"Shhhh. My concentration." He struggled to ease

the pants over her sneakers. "What's the matter here?"

"You should have taken the sneakers off first."

"First? . . . Oh. Okay. Sit down." With her pants bunched around her calves, she stumbled toward the chair. "Not there." He took her arm and propped her on the edge of the bed. "Here." Then he knelt to fumble with her laces. Several minutes later, sneakers, socks, and pants joined the top.

"Now." He stood and rubbed his hands together. "T-shirt." He reached for its hem then paused, squinted, and read its distorted message in disbelief. " 'Nurses like it in heavy doses'?"

"It was a joke." She pulled the shirt over her head, turning it inside out in the process, and tossed it aside. Only her underwear was left. Ben eyed it as though it were a final exam. He studied it, peered over her shoulder, stepped back, studied again. "Ben! I feel foolish!"

He held up a hand. "Uh-uh. I want to do it the right way. No fumbling in the dark this time. Eyes open, remember?"

"But you've seen it all before—"

"Not *this* way." Kneeling before her, he made ceremony of reaching for the front closing of her bra, slowly released it, as slowly unveiled its contents.

"Ben!" she whispered, more hoarse herself now with the cool air stroking her breasts.

"Almost there," he murmured distractedly. He reached to touch her, wavered in mid-air, withdrew with a taut clearing of his throat. "Stand up." She stood and he slid her panties off. Then, impulsively, he leaned forward and kissed her, sending a burst of sparks ricocheting among her nerve ends. Swaying, she reached to his head for balance.

"Ben! I can't take this!"

He looked up in innocence. "Should I stop?"

"Get *on* with it. My legs have been through hell today, and they'll only hold me so long." As it was, they were trembling badly.

He straightened. "Okay. Now . . . you."

"Me . . . what?"

"Undress me." He whisked his sweater up over his head. "There. I've given you a hand. Now you do my shirt."

"This is ridiculous," she muttered, but quickly released the buttons of his shirt, pulled it free of his slacks, and tugged it from his shoulders.

Her self-control couldn't compare with his; she didn't even try. The past two nights without him had left her starving. Without compunction, she slid her arms around his middle and drew herself close to savor the warmth of his skin. The contact of her breasts with his harder man's texture was electric.

"Abby . . ."

"Mmmmmm?"

"My pants, Abby. Hurry."

She moved her lips against his chest. "What's wrong, Ben? I thought we were taking this step by step."

"We are. But you're forgetting the steps."

"Wrong. This is a crucial step." Inhaling the scent that was his alone incited her all the more. She moved seductively against him, then drew a kiss out along his collarbone.

"Abby . . ."

She leaned back with a sigh. "Pants?"

"Pants."

Easily unbuckled, unzipped, removed. Shoes and socks likewise. When only his briefs remained, she stood on tiptoe and draped her arms over his shoulders. "Kiss me," she whispered, tipping up her face. His lips were no more than an inch away.

"You're not done—"

"Kiss me. Then I'll finish."

She could feel the taut control of his limbs, hear the ragged labor of his lungs. She knew he couldn't wait much longer.

His mouth opened, as did hers. Their lips touched lightly. His tongue traced the line of her teeth, then plunged deeper while he palmed her back and pressed her ever closer.

"I love you," he rasped when he finally paused to breathe. Then he made short work of the briefs himself, pulled down the quilt and set her back on the bed. "No blind impulses this time, Abby. You know what we're doing, don't you?" The pleading edge to his voice tugged at her heartstrings.

Looking up at him, she felt the surge of love through her veins. Her fingers smoothed the last of the furrows from his brow, then touched his eyes, his nose, his mouth. "I do know, Ben. We're making love."

He shook his head. "We're *loving* each other, babe, just as we've been doing all along. You said it once; you begged me to love you. Then I refused to acknowledge it. But no more. We're two thinking individuals; it's about time we know the facts."

"And Wyeth's Law?"

"Wyeth's Law has been repealed. Things are going to be different now—slow, logical, rational."

"Oh?" Smiling coyly, she stretched beneath him. Her hands slid down his body, outlining his hips before moving inward. When they reached their goal, they knew just what to do.

Ben moaned. "Maybe not slow . . ." Swallowing hard, he reached for her, and they were swept once again into the fiery vortex of passion. Heights of rapture later, they wondered about logical and rational too.

"I think I'll have to revise my thinking again," he

murmured sleepily. "There must be some compromise we can reach."

Content to lie against him, with the heat of their joining now a warm memory, Abby sighed softly. "We've reached it."

"Mmmmmmm." He shifted to draw up the quilt, then took her in his arms once more. "How about a honeymoon?"

"Sounds good."

"Now."

"When?"

"Tonight . . . tomorrow . . . Tuesday . . ."

"Don't you have to teach?"

"This is another emergency. Someone will cover for a couple more days. . . . How about you?"

She burrowed more snugly against his shoulder. "The worst of the colds and flu won't set in for another month. I think the office can survive without me for a few more days. . . . But I haven't any clothes!"

"None needed."

"Mmmmm."

They slept then, awakening later in the evening to call downstairs for room service. As they attacked a tray of hot steak sandwiches, chili, potato skins, fruit and wine, so they tackled those other topics they'd been unable to discuss earlier.

"Tell me about the deliberations, Ben. You refused to talk about them, and I didn't want to push. But I felt so left out, after all I went through. Was it as bad as you let on? Or were you just upset at having married me?"

"I was upset that you'd gotten to me so deeply. I needed to believe that I wasn't involved. Keeping my thoughts from you was one way. God, I was a bastard."

Abby raised her glass. "I'll drink to that."

Ben did as well, then grew serious. "The deliberations *were* terrible. It was one of the hardest things I've ever done . . . having to vote for a guilty."

"You didn't think he was?"

"I wasn't sure. There were several of us who felt that way. I'm afraid I held out the longest."

"It was your job, Ben. That's how our system works. But why . . . what held you back?"

"I sympathized with the guy! I knew how confused *I* was over *you.* There were times when I felt that *I'd* lost control of my senses. So who was I to say that Bradley couldn't have been temporarily insane?"

"What finally decided the issue?"

Sighing, he put down the last of his sandwich. "Love."

"Love?"

"I know that may sound whimsical in light of the gravity of the case. But in my mind the issue was whether Derek Bradley loved Greta Robinson. If he loved her, he might easily have been driven mad with wanting her and seeing her beyond his reach. God only knows *I* felt that way, and I wouldn't even admit to myself that I loved you!" Leaning across the tray, he pressed a gentle kiss to her lips. When he sat back, Abby eyed him smugly.

"The defense based its case on the theory of an irresistible impulse. What you're saying is that—"

"—*love* is an irresistible impulse. Those times during the trial, those nights we spent together, we may have simply thought we were being reckless . . . but we were wrong. There's a big difference between an *irresponsible* impulse and an *irresistible* impulse. What we did was in the name of love. There was nothing irresponsible about it." He grinned, ear to ear and winningly. "Irresistible, yes. Totally irresistible."

"I'll say." She mirrored his grin. "You *are* irresistible, you know that?" It was her turn to lean forward and kiss him, which she did both with due relish for his lips and due care for the tray between them. "We must make quite some picture," she remarked as if surveying the scene from afar. "Two adults who should know better, sitting on a bed wearing nothing but crumbs here and there . . . it's indecent!"

"It may be indecent, but you'd better get used to it." With that, he moved the tray to the table and returned to take her in his arms. "You'll have to be patient with me," he spoke more softly. "Now that I've accepted the fact of our love, I'm apt to be hopelessly possessive. If anything should happen to you—"

"Shhhhh. Nothing's going to happen."

"I'll do my best to make sure it doesn't!" He moved his mouth along her forehead. "You know something, Mrs. Wyeth?"

"Uh-uh. What?"

"You're pretty irresistible yourself."

"Oh?"

"Oh." End of conversation. This time, she had no complaints.

For an April storm, it was truly incredible. Snow conspired with wind to swirl heavy clusters of whiteness across the countryside.

Within, a warm fire blazed. Before it lay Ben, propped lazily on a bed of pillows, with Abby propped serenely on him. The howl of the wind and the crackle of the fire were an atmospheric accompaniment to their quiet intimacy.

"That was fun this afternoon," she said softly.

"Mmmm. Lucky the snow held off."

"I thought we were finished for the season."

He chuckled. "So did I. Not that I really minded those storms." They'd spent most of each one quite happily in each other's arms. "But it'll be easier for you when the warm weather comes."

"I'm fine now. The first three months are always the worst."

He held her closer. "Thank goodness." For a while the fire mesmerized them both. "It *was* nice today. They all looked wonderful."

"Even George with that . . . that . . ."

"Mustard tie?"

She laughed. "Poor guy. His taste is from hunger."

"Speaking of hunger, old Bernie put on quite a meal at that restaurant of his. Was it his idea to have the reunion?"

"I think it was Richard's. Then the two of them corralled Louise into contacting everyone." She paused to recall the joviality of the gathering. "Poor Patsy. She's *still* feeling lousy."

"When's she due?"

"In October, just about a month after I am."

"Damn good thing they got married when they did. Bud didn't waste any time."

She nudged him gently. "Neither did you, love."

"Nope."

They lay quietly then, with Ben's hand in restful possession of her stomach's slight bulge. "Brian asked about the book," Abby began softly. "He wanted to know if you were going ahead on it."

"What did you tell him?"

"I told him you were still gathering your thoughts."

"*We're* still gathering *our* thoughts. And it's really gone further than that. Brady should have a contract negotiated within the next week or two."

"I didn't want to tell Brian that. I think he's a little uptight about it anyway."

"I can see why . . . his image and all. I still have some doubts—"

"Do it, Ben! It's going to be a terrific study of the dynamics of a jury. It's not often that a skilled writer gets that kind of inside view."

Ben chuckled. "What was it I once said about your not pushing me? I take it back."

She ignored his teasing. "It's fascinating. I've thought so all along. I can remember that first day when they were strangers and so awkward with each other. To look at them now you'd think they'd known each other for years."

"You keep saying 'they.' Why not 'we'?"

" 'We' were never strangers. From the beginning there was something. . . ."

Tilting her face up, he dotted a kiss on the tip of her nose. "Right on!" Then he rubbed her belly once more. "You look so pretty."

"Isn't 'radiant' the customary word?"

"Could be. . . . Is this a maternity sweater?"

"Nope. Just a *big* sweater."

"You're not that big."

"Then why are all my clothes getting too tight? Besides, what better purpose for big sweaters than to cover up buttons that won't button!"

"Here, let me help." Reaching beneath the sweater, he located the button at her waist. But rather than trying to join it with its buttonhole, he lowered the zipper of her slacks and slid his hand beneath its soft wool to gently caress her.

"That feels nice," she purred.

"It does . . . small and round."

"You'll hate me when I get—"

"—I'll love you then too."

"You will?" An answer was superfluous when his hand strayed higher under the folds of her sweater. She sighed, then moaned when his fingers measured the greater fullness of her breasts.

"There'll just be more to love, that's all."

Looking up, she wound her arms around his neck. "You always know the right things to say."

"I try."

"You do, don't you. You've been so good about sharing things with me."

"I love you. You're my wife."

"But it wasn't always this way. Those first two weeks—"

"Shhhh." He put a finger over her lips. "That's long past."

"You're not still frightened?" It had been a while since she'd asked him.

"Sure I'm frightened. I wake up in the middle of the night sometimes in a panic if I don't feel you against me." He hesitated. "You do understand why I can't let you give birth to the baby here, don't you?"

It was something they'd discussed at length, something Abby would have loved to do. But she understood. And she was infinitely grateful that Ben could be honest with her, rather than bottling things up as he'd done at the start. "I do. And it's all right. As long as you're with me through the delivery . . . whether it's here or in the hospital."

He clutched her more tightly. "If anything should happen to you . . ."

"It won't, Ben. You'll see. Everything will be easy and very, very beautiful."

"You're very, very beautiful," he crooned, then kissed her thoroughly to prove his point. Wandering restlessly, his hands outlined her body. His touch held that same kind of tender possessiveness that never failed to move her.

"I love you," she whispered, arching closer.

"And I love you," he breathed, welcoming her fully. One kiss was followed by another, then another until their lips sought newer spots.

At its height their passion was strong, wild and reckless, a bounteous product of their love. It was their now, their tomorrow . . . unabashedly irresistible.